LAST STAND IN A DEAD LAND

by

Eric S. Brown

GRAND MAL
P R E S S

Published by:
Grand Mal Press
Forestdale, MA
www.grandmalpress.com

copyright 2011 Eric S. Brown

ISBN 13 digit: 9781937727000
ISBN 10 digit: 1937727009

Library of Congress Cataloging-in-Publication Data
Grand Mal Press/ Brown, Eric

p. cm

Cover art by Jade Moede

I would like to dedicate this book to A.P. Fuchs for keeping me writing, my son Merrick for his boundless imagination, and my wife for her constant support.

LAST STAND
IN A
DEAD LAND

PERFECTING THE DEAD

Eric S. Brown, or ESB as he's sometimes known to his fans, had become renowned for his heart-pumping, rollercoaster ride, never-lets-up fiction and I, like so many others, have become addicted to his special brand of horror. Eric, with all his forays into various sub-genres, has become something of a sub-genre himself. Mark my words, he will soon have imitators if he doesn't already.

And that, friends, is probably the highest compliment that can be paid to a writer.

I wish I could remember the first time I came across one of Eric's stories, but despite being unable to name exactly which one it was, I can tell you with utmost certainty the emotion I felt after reading it: exhilarated.

Here was a writer after my own heart. A minimalist who didn't bog the story down with unnecessary description. Instead, he shot it full of high octane adrenalin, grabbed the reader—me—by throat, stomped his foot on the gas and let out a good ole boy "YEEHAW!"

At least, that's what it felt like to me and if you've ever read any of his tales before, I know you know what I mean.

Eric has fun with his storytelling, which is always, always, how it should be with writers, and he almost dares you not to have fun yourself. And that is a challenge you should not accept, because you will lose.

It is impossible to not have fun with an ESB tale and *Last Stand in a Dead Land* is no exception.

— Gina Ranalli

PART I: Survivors

PART II
SURVIVORS

The smell of rotting meat was the worst part of it. It made Jacob sick to his stomach and nothing he had tried so far helped to shut it out. Tying a cloth over his mouth and nose was pointless. It didn't even begin to filter the odor out. That stuff about Vick's Vapor Rub was a load of crap too. Oh, it worked but only for a few seconds. Unless you continued to slather it on every couple of minutes or held your nose directly into the jar, the help it gave faded away too quickly. Jacob had thought one's sense of smell was supposed to adapt to odors and get used to them to the point where one didn't even know they were there. Two days had passed and he was still waiting for that to happen too. Two days. The thought of that freaked him out. Two days and no help had come. Two days of living off potato chips, candy bars, and peanuts, drinking toilet water since the bottled water vending machine had been empty like it normally was at the end of a workday, and no internet. The world had really gone to Hell in the blink of an eye.

Jacob sat against the wall in the space between two of the vending machines. It was crazy hot. The power had gone out that first night when they came and never come back on. He remembered being stupid enough to offer to stay late and help Daniel with the last of the edits on the latest issue of *Croatoan*. That one act of kindness had either cost him his life or saved it. He wasn't sure which. The television and the web, before the power went out, had been filled with reports of some kind of virus sweeping through the city. He and Daniel cracked Night of the Living Dead jokes about it while they worked. Everything was fine that morning as they'd come to work. Neither of them really believed the apocalypse could unfold in a matter of hours. It wasn't until the elevator doors opened and nine, snarling things that once were human beings came pouring out of it that they had believed. Of course, by then, it was too late. Daniel tried to fight the things and paid the price for it. Jacob sealed himself up in the break room, locking and barricading the door. He'd been here ever since. He'd heard Daniel's screams as the man had died and the far worse sounds of the meal the things partook of afterwards.

He didn't doubt that at least a few of the things were still in the office, waiting on him to come out or die. Occasionally, at random intervals, one of them would attack the break room's door, pounding its rotting fists against it with such fury Jacob could only pray the door would hold and try not to pee his pants every time it happened. Usually, after a few minutes, the thing would give up and go back to wandering aimlessly around or whatever it was they were doing out there.

Jacob hauled himself to his feet, making his way across the room to its sole window. He'd smashed it open with a chair in desperation earlier, before what little rationality he retained convinced him in desperation it would be suicide to make any kind of escape attempt through it. This was real life, not the movies, even if it felt as if he was stuck in a bad horror flick. Jacob leaned through it to look at the street. A few of the dead roamed about amid the wrecked and abandoned cars below. Their numbers grew smaller every time he did this. His best guess was that the things were moving on to other hunting grounds, which meant they had picked this area of the city clean of survivors, except for maybe other folks who were hopelessly trapped like he was. Jacob refused to believe he was the last person left alive in the entire city. That just couldn't be possible.

Jacob knew he needed a plan but he was stuck on the seventh floor of an office building with no real weapons or even rope, surrounded by a city full of the living dead. He headed back over to the door and pressed his ear against it. Maybe, just maybe with a bit of luck, he could make it past the ones in the office. Then he'd do what he always did as a writer: Make stuff up as he went along.

There was some kind of commotion happening in the office, the worst he had heard since that first day. Something was definitely getting the dead riled up. He heard a moan followed by several snarls. There was a series of "ppfftt" sounds then only silence. He took a step away from the door not quite sure what to do.

"Come on and open the door," a man's voice called to him. "We ain't got all day."

Jacob stared at the door in utter shock and disbelief. Finally, he managed to say, "Who. . . Who are you?"

"I ain't the Grim Reaper, kid, if that's what you're wondering. He seems to be taking a vacation these days."

Jacob laughed in spite of himself. Something about the man's gruff and self assured tone put him at ease. "Okay, hold on."

Jacob shoved his makeshift barricade at the base of the door aside and unlocked it. The man outside stood in the middle of a sea of overturned desks, loose papers blowing in the breeze from one of the huge, shattered office windows, with a gun in his hand and two corpses at his feet. A long silencer was attached to the gun's barrel explaining the odd noises he'd heard.

The man looked like some kind of hero from a post-apocalyptic movie. He wore a long, gray trench coat and Jacob could see several more weapons buried within its pockets. The hilt of a sword stuck out above the top of the backpack he wore, over his left shoulder. A touch of gray marked his otherwise jet black hair and a set of strange goggles covered his eyes.

"Seriously, man," Jacob asked, "Who in the Hades are you?"

"A survivor, just like you. Now we gotta move. Whether they heard me or not, those things can smell us. Move it!" The man turned and ran for the elevator.

"Those don't work!" Jacob told him, but even as he said the words, he saw that the elevator's door was open. Metal cables glinted in the darkness inside the shaft. The man tossed him a pair of thick gloves.

"Hope you can climb. The stairwells are a bit occupied."

Jacob pulled the gloves on, said a prayer, and leaped for the closest cable as seven more snarling corpses burst into the office area.

Jacob tried not to look down as he worked his way towards the building's lobby. His arms ached and sweat drenched his hair, dripping into and stinging his eyes. By the time the two of them reached the second floor, Jacob was beginning to wonder if starving to death, all alone in the break room, might have been the better option.

"This is where we get off," the man informed him. "Too many of them on the ground floor."

Finding the courage to look down, Jacob saw

dozens of hungry faces staring up at them from the bottom of the elevator shaft as the man pulled a small crossbow device from his trench coat and fired a bolt at the shaft's wall. It struck the wall with a loud thud. There was some kind of thin climbing wire attached to it. The man let go of the cable and swung over to the elevator door of the second floor. Bracing himself against the wall, the man strained and shoved them open. A dead woman came tumbling towards him as Jacob watched. The man swung from her path as the rotter's hands grabbed for him and missed. She landed somewhere below with a crashing thump. The man swung back to the open door and vanished through it. A full minute later, he reappeared, extending a hand. "It's the only way, kid. I got you."

Jacob threw himself at the man, who caught his hand and yanked him into the second floor corridor. Rubbing at his arm muscles, Jacob leaned against the wall, catching his breath. "That was some hardcore Batman stuff."

"Thanks," the man said, "I wasn't entirely sure it would work to be honest."

Jacob suddenly felt very sick at his stomach. "You didn't tell me your name."

"Elijah," the man said, his gaze focused on the other end of the hallway where the stairwell was. "I have a van parked in the street on the north side. Hope you're ready for a good run because the easy part's over with."

"The easy part?" Jacob made a face at him wondering if Elijah was completely insane.

Elijah drew a pistol from a holster beneath his trench coat and handed it to him. "The safety's off. You only got seventeen shots so make them count if you have to use it."

"My gun doesn't have a silencer," Jacob commented.

"I said run, didn't I?"

Elijah and Jacob ran through the hallway at a full out sprint with Elijah in the lead. As they neared the midway point of the hall, the doorway to an office burst open and tall man in a tattered and blood-stained business suit sprang into their path. Yellow teeth flashed as the thing took a bite at Elijah's left shoulder. Elijah met its attempt with a gloved fist to its face that sent teeth flying and caved in the thing's nose. The dead man staggered backwards a few steps, moaning, before Elijah leveled his pistol at its forehead and sent it back to Hell. The thing's skull exploded like a blood-filled water balloon.

Elijah skidded to a halt in front of a door near the hallway's end and kicked it open with one of his heavy boots. "This way!"

Jacob watched him barrel across the room and jump out the already smashed window inside. He ran to its edge and looked down to see Elijah standing on top of a black van, a pistol in each hand, blazing away at a pack of dead who were already closing in to surround it. Jacob raised his own pistol and started shooting from where he stood.

"Forget it, you idiot!" Elijah yelled at him. "Just

bloody freaking jump!"

Elijah slid himself into the van's driver seat and its engine roared to life as Jacob leapt for his life. He landed painfully, his right cheek smacking against the van's metal roof. With almost no time to recover, Jacob fought to hold on as Elijah kicked the van into gear and floored the gas. The van plowed through and over the closest of the dead. Blood and pus splattered into the air.

"Yeah!" Jacob heard Elijah yell as they hit the freeway and the bulk of the dead shrank into the distance behind them.

An eternity-seeming rough ten minutes went by before Elijah ever stopped to let Jacob get off the roof and into the van. Jacob stared in awe at the stockpile of weapons and supplies covering the floor of its back. "Did you rob a bloody military base?"

Elijah ignored him as the moaning of the dead filled the street. The alley they had parked in quickly began to fill up with the dead. The things were drawn to the sound of the van's engines like flies to a pile of poop. Jacob turned to Elijah, "So, uh, you do have a plan right?"

"Sure. A pretty simple one too."

"Mind cluing me in?"

"Save everyone I can and get the Hell out of this city before we become corpse food."

"Great plan. I've told you you're crazy right?"

Elijah laughed.

"How exactly did you find me anyhow?" Jacob asked.

Elijah produced a small, handheld device from one of his many pockets and showed it to him. "Life detector you could call it, I guess. It's experimental military tech."

Jacob shrugged. "Sure, why not? If the dead can walk, anything's possible. So where are we headed now?"

Elijah's only answer was a grin that sent a shiver through Jacob's spine.

Lori screamed as the window's glass shattered and a pair of loose skinned, rotting hands grabbed at her. She backpedaled away, tripping over the living room rug, landing on her butt and grunting from the pain. The hardwood floor wasn't kind to her posterior. The dead teenager tore away the final nailed-in-place board with the help of two other rotters and began to haul itself through the window at her.

"Michael!" Lori yelled. "They're inside!"

She scrambled to her feet and bolted for the basement door. Michael met her there, a pump action shotgun in his hands.

"I told you not to come up here," he grumbled. "Now we're really going to be trapped downstairs."

"As if we weren't anyway," Lori snapped at him, just as the teenager flopped onto the hardwood floor below the window. Another rotter was already climbing through the broken window after it.

Michael raised the shotgun but Lori slapped its barrel down towards the floor. "Don't use it unless we have to," she warned him. "Remember last time?"

Whether he did or not, Lori blamed the horde of creatures in the yard on him. The first time they had tried to leave the house, it had been his genius plan to try to fight their way to the car sitting in their driveway. It hadn't worked out very well for them. As soon as he had stopped to reload, they had been forced to hightail it back inside and within minutes the number of rotters outside had tripled. She guessed there were at least fifty of the things around the house now and the makeshift fortifications were finally starting to crumble from the things' relentless attacks. Lori put her hand on Michael's chest and shoved him through the basement door. She saw him start to protest but cut him off. "We can't fight them all, Michael, and you know it. You've got what, maybe two dozen shells left?"

The dead teenage boy was on his feet and he came charging towards them. Lori slammed the door in his face and together she and Michael held it closed as he raged against it on the other side.

"So what now?" Michael demanded.

"Get the board in place!" Lori shouted at him.

The two of them had rigged up an old fashioned katy bar for the door. Michael reached for the board with one hand, keeping his other in place to help her. Finally, they got it in place. Lori watched the door shake in its frame as more of the dead joined the teenager. She could hear several distinct hungry cries coming from the other side now.

"It's not going to hold them," she admitted.

"Not for long anyway," Michael agreed.

"Well, I for one am not giving up without a fight," she told him and darted down the steps.

They only had the one gun so she snatched up a metal baseball bat from where it lay propped on the side of the washing machine and got ready. Michael moved to stand by her side.

"Look. . .I'm sorry," he said.

"Not the time," Lori said through clenched teeth as the door above them splintered and three rotters came half rolling, half bouncing down the steps. Lori didn't give them a chance to recover from their fall. She sprang forward, caving in the closest one's skull with a vicious swing as it looked up at her with soulless, hollow eyes. She bashed it two more times as Michael's shotgun thundered, echoing off the cement walls, turning one of the rotter's faces into reddish pulp.

"Watch out!" she howled as the third rotter, not bothering to get up from where it had landed, latched onto Michael's leg with its right hand. Michael swung the butt of his shotgun downwards onto the top of its black hair with the sickening sound of bone caving inward.

Seven more rotters had already taken the place of the first three and this time the things were on their feet and closing in fast. Lori met one with a swing that broke its jaw and sent it reeling into the others. The sound of gunfire erupted from somewhere above. Lori and Michael exchanged a "what in the Hades" glance at each other.

"Hold on! We're coming!" Someone called to them from upstairs. A nerdy looking guy in a Flash shirt appeared at the top of the steps behind the rotters. He fired three times with the 9mm pistol in his hand, knocking one of the rotters from its feet. A real weirdo, dressed like he'd just walked off the set of a low budget science fiction movie, came flying past the nerd into the rotters. The bloody blade of his katanna took the head of one of the creatures. Before the things could barely move, he'd gutted a second, causing it to trip over its own intestines, and slashed open a third's head, splattering the basement wall with black pus and brain matter.

Suddenly, filled with hope that she'd live to see the next sunrise, Lori let loose a battle cry and rejoined the fray as Michael pumped off another round. The nerdy guy leaned over the steps' railing to press the barrel of his pistol against the backside of a rotter's head and squeezed the trigger. The rotter's forehead exploded outward, its twitching form collapsing to the floor. The last of the rotters in the basement met its end as the weirdo's katanna sent the top half of its head tumbling towards Lori.

"I'm Jacob. That freaky guy is Elijah. We're here to save you," the nerdy guy said.

Elijah bounded up the steps, out of the basement, like a cat. His movements smooth but hurried. Jacob gave them a weak smile.

"Stop standing there!" Lori yelled at him. She rushed past Jacob with Michael on her heels. The living room was a war zone. The front door was smashed in, likely from where Jacob and Elijah had entered, and a dozen or more of the rotters filled the room.

Lori saw Elijah sheath his sword, drawing two Glocks from holsters underneath the trench coat he wore. Elijah ran at the rotters and through them, his guns blazing. Only three remained by the time he had disappeared into the yard. Lori heard Michael's shotgun boom behind her. A rotter took its blast full on in the chest and went sprawling over the living room couch. Lori ran at the last one in her path to the door as Michael dropped the other remaining creature with a pair of quick shots that shattered one of its legs and blew off chunks of its right shoulder. *That's my husband,* she thought, *Couldn't land a headshot anymore than he could hit the broad side of a barn.* But she knew the creature wouldn't be getting up until they were long gone.

The rotter in her path was a man in the blue shirt and khaki shorts of a mailman. A sack of letters still dangled, forgotten, in a bag strapped over his left shoulder. He had been mauled, badly. There wasn't much left of his neck to speak of. *Easy,* she thought, rearing back her bat, but the dead man surprised her. He sprang at her with an inhuman speed, driven by insatiable hunger. He somehow managed to block her bat as she brought it around, knocking it from her grasp. Lori's eyes went wide with fear as his cold hands clamped onto her arms. His chomping teeth shot forward at her flesh. A pistol cracked and the dead man's eye imploded as a 9mm round dug through it into his brain, snapping his head away from her. The motion ripped apart what little sinew remained holding it to his body. Lori screamed and kicked the severed head that had fallen to her feet across the room before getting a grip on her situation again. She hopped over the headless corpse where it lay in her path and dashed out the front door. Elijah was waiting there in a van with the motor running. She dove through its open side door into its back.

As soon as Michael and Jacob made it into the van, Elijah floored the gas. The van smashed through the short, white fence lining the house's yard and kept right on going.

"Wouldn't happen to have any Oreos on you, would ya?" Elijah asked without taking his eyes from the road ahead and the rotters racing to meet them.

"Nope," Lori answered, "fresh out."

She saw that Michael and Jacob were as stunned by the bizarre question as she was.

"Too bad," Elijah said, jerking the steering wheel around to dodge an abandoned Ford Taurus sitting in the middle of the road. "I could really go for some right now."

As they drove, Jacob explained how Elijah had saved him as well and gave them a rundown on the plan, if it could be called that. They were as awestruck by the insanity of it all initially just as he had been but Jacob had learned to just roll with Elijah's craziness. If it kept him alive, it couldn't be a bad thing, could it? Still, Jacob was happy to have Lori and Michael with them. The married couple sat across from him in the rear of the van, holding hands as the three of them traded stories and talked.

"Any idea how all this started?" Jacob asked them. "I didn't really keep up with the news. . .back when there was news."

"I figured you guys would know a lot more than we do," Michael told him.

"I don't know anything," Jacob confessed, "I heard there was a virus and that's all."

"We heard that too," Lori said as she undid her ponytail, fluffing waves of long, brown hair over her shoulders.

Jacob hoped Michael didn't notice him checking her out. She was cute in an odd kind of way. Her body was super thin but well-toned, her breasts surprisingly large for such a lithe frame. The tight, white tank top she wore made it hard not to stare in spite of the red and black stains covering it. Her eyes were a fierce green, sharp and strong. The features of her face were angular like a bird's. Michael, on the other hand, was nothing to write home about. He was your typical, big, hulking jock. Jacob would never want to go head to head with him in a straight up fight but was otherwise utterly unimpressed by the man. It was easy to picture Michael talking sports, going hunting, and lifting weights in the basement of the house he and Lori shared. He seemed the kind of guy Jacob and his friends had always mocked and made fun of. Quite honestly, Jacob wondered what Lori saw in him. Jacob knew he had let his gaze linger a bit too long on Lori's chest as Michael cleared his throat.

"I don't want to come across as ungrateful," the big man said, "But we've got family out there."

"No!" Elijah chimed in from the driver's seat. "You don't. They're dead. The sooner you accept that the better. We stay together or you will be too."

"Now look!" Michael's voice rose as his cheeks flashed red with sudden anger. "You can't possibly know that."

"No, Michael," Lori said as Jacob watched her squeeze his hand. "Elijah's right. The world is dead. Everything we knew, everyone we knew, is gone."

Michael slumped where he sat, clearly defeated. Jacob marveled at the little woman's power over the giant but wondered if he would be any different in the big man's place.

"The only questions we should be asking are how to stay alive and how to start over," Lori said. "This is all just so much to deal with."

"You got that part right," Michael grunted.

Lori turned towards the front of the van. "Mr. Elijah, how many more people are you planning on trying to save?"

Jacob smiled. She really did go straight for the heart of things. She'd just put Elijah on the spot with a direct question he had to answer or risk losing them all.

"There are two more places that I know of," Elijah said. "There's a police station where a small group of folks seem to be holding their own against the dead. They've been doing okay so far, however, I doubt it will go well for them when their ammo begins to run out. There's also another sole survivor reading registering in the warehouse district, inside of what appears to be the city morgue according to my map."

Jacob stared at Elijah. "There's a whole other group of people still alive? Why in the Hades didn't we go to them first?"

"If we had, Jacob, would Lori and Michael be alive at this moment?" Elijah countered.

Jacob noticed the married couple staring at him. "I didn't mean. . ."

"It's okay," Lori assured him. "So which one do we go after, Elijah?"

"The lone reading, of course. That person is the least likely to survive without our help. Besides, the group at the police station would bring too many problems with them."

"Afraid they'd stick you in a home for special people again?" Michael mocked him.

"Man, that was a low blow," Jacob shook his head.

Elijah was untroubled by Michael's insult so far as Jacob could tell.

"I never said I was in an asylum, Michael."

"That's the point," Michael said, "you haven't told us crap about who you are or where you came from. Where did you get all these weapons and ammo much less that. . .that thing you're using to find people? How did you survive the first night?"

Elijah suddenly hit the brakes. The van squealed to a halt in the center of the road. The cries of the nearby dead rose in pitch as they scurried to take advantage of what might be their only chance at a meal anytime soon.

"You are welcome to go your own way if I disturb you that much, Michael." Elijah's voice was cold and firm.

Jacob hopped from his seat, moving to peek through the van's front window over Elijah's shoulder. Five rotters were closing in on the van and those were just the ones Jacob could see. "Elijah, what are you doing, man?" Jacob whispered.

Lori jumped as a pair of dead, gray hands slapped against the windows of the van's rear door.

"Get us moving!" she yelled at Elijah.

He ignored her, sitting calmly behind the wheel, his attention focused solely on Michael.

"Fine!" Michael roared, throwing his hands in the air in gesture of surrender. "Keep your secrets. Just get us out of here."

Elijah grinned and stepped on the gas. The van hurled forward through the rotters. "Michael," Elijah said quietly as he drove, "don't ever imply that I am crazy again."

Jacob breathed a sigh of relief, returning to his seat. "Well," he said, "let's go be heroes again," in an attempt to ease the tension that still hung in the air.

As Elijah steered the van through the rubble of the city streets to the morgue, Jacob thought about the folks holed up at the police station and began to understand why Elijah really didn't want to go there. If those folks were doing okay, even if just for the time being, they may not want company. To them, a new little group might appear as nothing more than more mouths to try to feed, or worse, a threat. An encounter with Jacob's group could lead to all kinds of trouble. The police station crew could force them to stay, thinking they were doing them a favor, or try to take what they had as their own to buy themselves another day or two of being able to stand against the dead. . . And those scenarios assumed that they would be willing to talk at all. They might just try to defend their turf outright and greet them with bullets. At least the rotters didn't shoot back at you. Those folks certainly could if it came to that.

Jacob also thought about his own family and friends. Trapped in his office's break room, he had hoped that some of them were still alive. Having seen what the city had become with his own eyes, those hopes were gone. Jacob had always been kind of a loner and his parents were long dead from a car accident five years ago. The few friends he did have were close ones, even his ex-girlfriend. He thought about Keith at the comic shop, Kristen in her apartment, Shawn working at a construction site and hoped their deaths were easy ones, that they had all died quickly without much pain. It was unlikely but it was the best he could do for them now. He looked up to see that Michael had fallen asleep where he sat. The big man snored softly, his head hanging over his chest.

"Got any water?" Lori asked, pulling Jacob from his thoughts.

The van was packed with all sorts of supplies and weapons. Jacob was sure he had seen a case or two of bottled water somewhere in the mess. He dug about trying to find a bottle. "I'm pretty sure we do," he said. "Sorry. I should have offered you guys something sooner. Elijah isn't exactly the most considerate host, eh?"

Lori smiled at him. "No worries," she said, "Without him, we would all be dead. I think we can cut him some slack where manners are concerned."

"He's listening, ya know?" Jacob teased her, cocking his head towards the front of the van. "Try not to give him any more of a hero complex than he's already got."

Jacob found the water and handed a bottle to Lori. She twisted the top off and drank half of it before lowering the bottle from her lips. "Thanks," she said with a smile that made Jacob feel hot and woozy.

Jacob fought away the sparks stirring within

him and tore his eyes away from her.

Mark was having a blast. The apocalypse had been the best thing that ever happened to him so far. He was a self-made king in this new world of hungry corpses and anarchy. The morgue's heavy steel door kept the dead at bay and he had stock-piled the place full of everything he thought he would need, and then some, while everyone else was still refusing to believe the end had come. Heck, the morgue even had its own generator. Used care-fully, his supply of gas would last weeks. By then maybe the monsters would have rotted away. Who knew? He plopped the chainsaw onto the autopsy table, filling its tank from a jug of gasoline. A loud thump sounded from inside one of the refrigerated corpse storage units in the wall.

"Shut up!" he shouted. "I'll deal with you later!"

Mark lifted the chainsaw and marched over to the morgue's side door. Unlike the main entrance, it was made of wood but it was thick and tough. It led into the chapel area which was the only true in-secure part of his domain. He had fortified it as best he could before the dead swarmed the area around the building. Mark carefully cracked the side door, peeping into the chapel. A chorus of moans, snarls, and grunts could be heard from within but he didn't see any rotters that had made it inside among the pews. Scores upon scores of arms covered in green and gray decaying flesh flailed about through and in between the boards he had nailed in place over the sea of windows. Oh yeah, he thought, it's fun time. He cranked up the chainsaw and went to work.

Ten minutes later, covered in blood and black pus, he staggered into the morgue proper again. Most of the rotters were missing their arms or, at the very least, their hands from his efforts. It lowered their chances of tearing away the boards and getting inside, or so he told himself. The things were packed so thickly outside that the ones close enough to get their arms in were actually pressed against the walls by the weight of those behind them to where they could barely move. It should be a while until the crowd of them, as brainless as the things were, shifted around enough to be a threat again.

The one thing the morgue lacked was a shower. Mark stripped away his soiled clothing, cleaning himself with pieces of a torn-up lab coat at one of the larger sinks. Then he put his clothes in it to soak for a while before he attempted to wash them. Shrugging on a long lab coat over his otherwise naked body, he grabbed a beer from one of the morgue's large freezers and sat down at the work desk in the main room. Patting himself on the back for a job well done, he took a sip of the beer and opened the laptop in front of him. When he had moved in, he had wired several security cameras along the edges of the roof so he could keep a better eye on the building's exterior. He watched hundreds of corpses on a laptop now, wandering about the parking lot and the streets beyond it. The sight of the things reminded him of the ones stored in the morgue when he had first arrived. Dealing with those fraggers hadn't been fun. Unlike the ones trying to get into the chapel, they had been able to fight him. Only the devil knew how much ammo he'd wasted blowing them into twitching pieces. If he ever had to do all this again, Mark swore he would leave the creatures more intact next time. Cleaning up that mess took forever. A thump sounded from one of the roll out corpse containers in the wall again.

"I told you to shut up!" he raged, walking over to it and pounding his fist loudly on its small, square door. "Can't a man get a second to kick back with a beer and think?"

The noise stopped. Marked returned to his seat, still grumbling quietly under his breath. "What in the Hades?" he spat out a mouthful of his beer as he watched a black van come tearing into the morgue's parking lot. Its side door was open and some idiot leaned out from it with the biggest machine gun Mark had ever seen, mowing down the rotters as the van drove around in circles. Mark suddenly felt very cold. For the first time in his three days of paradise, his perfect little home was truly threatened. Whoever those folks in the van were, whether they made it past the rotters or not, he wasn't about to let them in. He realized what they were doing as he continued to watch them on the laptop's screen. They weren't trying to kill all the creatures, merely thin the things' ranks enough to make for the chapel door, his door. Mark didn't bother to put on anything else. With his lab coat open and his male parts flopping about freely, he grabbed his closest weapon and got ready to meet them just in case.

Michael hosed the rotters in the parking lot, keeping the M-60's trigger squeezed tight. Hot, spent casings bounced against the side of the van and its floor. Jacob stayed near him, pistol ready in hand, trying to make sure the heavy weapon's belt didn't jam. Elijah sat behind them with some kind assault rifle cradled in his lap. Jacob was shocked when Elijah had asked Lori to take the wheel but he supposed she was the best choice. Jacob didn't even have a license. With all the public transit in the city, he had never needed one. Like sports, cars just weren't his thing.

A dead woman in a wedding dress came howling towards the van and into Michael's stream of continuous fire. Rounds from the M-60 pulped the upper half of her body like a slab of meat being tossed into a grinder. Jacob guessed most of the dead would still be alive, for lack of a better word, when they were done but they would be so mangled it wouldn't matter. Elijah's plan would get them inside the morgue.

Michael swung the heavy gun at a pack of dead blocking their path to the chapel door. One of the things was cut nearly in half, intestines spewing as its body twisted from the bullets' impact. The others around it took more rounds than Jacob could guess at, collapsing into bloodied and shattered heaps on the chapel steps.

Lori spun the van, bringing the M-60 around to face the newer rotters still emerging from the alleyways beyond the parking lot.

"It's not going to get any better," Jacob heard Elijah say loudly over the roar of the van's engine and the chatter of the gunfire. "It's time to do this."

Michael looked relieved. His hair was drenched with sweat and he wore a pained expression. The big man dropped the weapon. It clattered to the asphalt as Lori aimed the van at the chapel. Jacob was impressed as she went further than any of them expected.

"Get down!" she yelled as the van plunged through the chapel's wall. Jacob and Michael held on for dear life, the initial impact almost sending them flying. The van came to rest with its hood touching the rear row of pews. Elijah was out of the side door like lightning.

"I'll hold them here! Find the survivor!" he ordered them.

Despite all the weapons Elijah had for them to choose from, Michael clutched his own shotgun as he leapt from the van, his pockets were now overflowing with additional shells. Jacob stuck with the pistol Elijah had given him when they met. Lori, however, wore a pistol holstered on a belt around her waist and carried twin UZIs in her hands, all looted from Elijah's stash.

There was a heavy wooden door to the right side of the chapel's interior that appeared to lead into the morgue. Lori beat everyone to it as Jacob gave Elijah a final glance before following after her. Elijah's job was made easier by the van acting as a dam against the flood of rotters; they were forced to wedge themselves around it through the small openings in the chapel's walls by its sides.

"It's locked!" Lori shouted as she clubbed the door with the butt of one of her UZIs.

"Step aside!" Jacob heard Michael order her. The big man raised his shotgun, aiming for the lock.

"Wait!" Jacob told them as he caught up. "I got this one!"

He fished a paperclip from the pocket of his jeans.

"You're telling me you know how to pick a lock?" Michael said.

"I thought you were a writer," Lori added.

"What can I say?" Jacob laughed as he went to work. "I got into a butt load of trouble as a lad."

A loud click sounded and Jacob shoved the door inward. A flash erupted from the hallway beyond it as a double barreled shotgun sent death flying at him. Only a mix of Jacob being crouched at the level of the lock and his terrified state saved him. He ducked forward, rolling into the morgue as the slugs streaked over him. Michael wasn't so lucky. Jacob heard the big man scream but had no time to check on him. The door had been booby trapped and something told Jacob whoever set it wouldn't be happy to see them. Jacob started to get to his feet as the blade of an ax came swinging at his head. He let out a yelp, throwing himself back to the floor. The blade buried itself in the wall above him. A man wearing only a lab coat and nothing more strained to yank it free for another go at him. Lori stepped into the doorway, her UZIs chattering. The nearly naked man managed to dodge the bulk of her fire by ducking around a corner but Jacob saw him take a bullet in his arm. Blood sprayed onto white as the man vanished from sight.

"What do we do?" Lori asked as Jacob lay at her feet.

"Hades if I know!" he yelled. "Is Michael okay?"

"He's alive," Lori said. She kept her gaze focused on the bend in the hallway where the man had disappeared.

Jacob scrambled up from the floor. "We could really use Elijah's help here," he commented.

"Elijah's kind of busy." Lori took a couple of steps forward. "We're gonna have to handle this ourselves."

"Mister!" Jacob screamed. "We're not here to hurt you! We just want to help!"

"Go away, you fraggers!" a voice shouted. "We

don't need your help!"

"We?" Lori mouthed at Jacob.

"Okay," Jacob said, "This guy is starting to make Elijah look sane."

"Your trap blew a hole in my husband!" Lori yelled. "Either show yourself so we can talk or we're coming in!"

Only silence answered her.

"Ladies first?" Jacob said weakly. The glare Lori shot him let him know how many rungs on her ladder of respect he had just plummeted. "Fine," he grumbled. If he was really doing this, he was doing it Elijah style. Jacob unleashed a sad joke of a battle cry and ran headlong towards the bend in the hallway. The sheer insanity of his action took everyone off guard, including the naked man in the lab coat. As Jacob rounded the corner, the man was in the process of fiddling with the shotgun he'd snatched from the trap he had set, trying to reload it. Jacob and the naked man stared at each other in wide-eyed horror. Jacob moved faster, kicking the man in the groin. The naked man grunted, bending over at the waist, then Jacob was on him. Tearing the weapon from his hands and flinging it aside, Jacob plowed into the man like a professional football player. The two of them crashed into the wall, the naked man taking the brunt of their impact before they careened over into the floor.

Jacob landed on top, struggling to hold the man under him. "We're here to help you!" Jacob pleaded. "There's no need for any of this!"

The man slammed his forehead into Jacob's face. Jacob's world became one of pain. The man threw Jacob to the right, turning the tables on him. A long strand of saliva dripped from his mouth over Jacob's eyes as the man clutched Jacob's wrists, pinning his arms to the floor above his head.

"I told you to leave!" the man growled like a mad dog, "I don't want your help!"

Jacob didn't notice Lori's approach until the butt of one of her UZIs made contact with the backside of the man's skull. His eyes rolled up to show only whites from the blow before he toppled forward. Jacob shoved his unconscious form aside. "I don't care what Elijah says, we're not taking this guy with us!" Jacob said wiping the man's spit from his eyes and cheek with the back of his hand.

A frantic thumping noise drew Jacob's attention towards the morgue's main room.

"What in the devil is that?" Lori asked.

"Surely the whacko wouldn't have locked one of those things in here with him, right?"

"We're here," Lori told him, "might as well check it out."

Jacob and Lori discovered the noise was coming from one of the slideout corpse storage units in the room's wall. Jacob knew she wasn't going to leave without taking a look inside it. He placed a hand on its lock. "You ready?" he asked, knowing he wasn't.

"Do it!" Lori ordered him, her UZIs aimed at the door of the unit.

Jacob threw the lock, jumping away as he slid the slab out from the wall.

"Holy. . .!" Lori screamed. A teenage girl with pale skin, dressed in a torn black teddy, lay on the slab. Deep, purple bruises covered her cheeks and the flesh of her thighs. Her hands and feet were bloodied and battered things, likely from her continued attempts to free herself from her tight, metal prison.

"Help me," the girl groaned weakly at Lori.

"Oh, honey," Lori sobbed, helping the poor girl to sit up.

"Yep," Jacob said, "I am so putting a bullet in that guy's brain on the way out. No question about it."

As Jacob turned to leave the morgue and Lori was beginning to ease the girl onto her feet, a fist met his jaw like a sledgehammer. Jacob staggered, barely managing to stay on his feet as the room spun around him.

"You ain't doing no such thing," the naked man smiled, his good arm holding the shotgun from the trap at Lori and the girl. "Thanks for leaving this here gun behind. Had a couple of shells for it in the pocket of this coat. Got a pretty good idea how I'll use them too."

"Do you?" Elijah's voice echoed in the room as he stepped into it. He was carrying Michael, or rather dragging him, with the big man's arm over his shoulders.

"For Heaven's sake!" the naked man complained. "How many of you losers are there?"

Jacob watched Elijah's wrist flick. A silver throwing knife imbedded itself in the naked guy's hand, jerking it to the side as the double barreled shotgun thundered. The blast went wide of Lori and the girl, its slugs sparking off the wall beside them. A second knife caught the naked man in his forehead, sinking deep into his brain. A tiny trickle of blood formed below where the knife protruded from his flesh. He stumbled towards Jacob and fell over face first into the floor at his feet.

"What are you doing here?" Jacob asked as Elijah dropped Michael and moved to close the heavy wooden side door.

"You took too long," Elijah said. "I couldn't hold the rotters any longer."

"So does that mean. . ." Lori started, already moving to Michael's side.

Jacob's heart sank as Elijah answered, "Yes. We're trapped."

Michael sat propped up in a chair. His skin a greenish hue and his expression contorted into a mask of pain as Elijah finished bandaging his stomach. Lori knew he needed her. She loved Michael but she also knew the girl needed her more. She wouldn't let any of the guys get close to her, not without it freaking her out, so Lori took charge of her care. The girl sat in another chair, across the room from Michael, as Lori knelt beside her. Lori wanted desperately to get a better look at the girl's hands and feet to see how bad they really were but the girl wouldn't even let Lori touch her yet. "What's your name?" Lori whispered gently.

"Helena," the teen whimpered. Helena cocked her head to where Jacob placed the psycho in the lab coat's body underneath a sheer, black plastic cover. "He's really dead? He's not coming back?"

Lori shook her head. "No, he's dead for real. No one is going to hurt you anymore."

Helena leaned into her, arms wrapping around Lori in an embrace. Jacob was pacing the length of the morgue's main room, muttering to himself. Lori did her best to ignore him. "Helena, can you run?"

The girl nodded. She offered Lori one of her hands. "They look worse than they are."

A lab coat, like the man wore, was all they could find to cloth Helena with. Lori made a mental note to try to find the girl some shoes as soon as they could.

"Your friend," Helena said cautiously, "is he okay?"

"Huh?" Lori wasn't sure who the girl meant.

"He keeps talking to himself," Helena explained.

At that moment, Jacob must have snapped. "Dang it!" he screamed. "I didn't go through all this to be trapped again, Elijah! How in the Hades are we gonna get out of here?" Jacob walked closer to the morgue's side door, smashing his fist into it.

"Come on, Elijah! What's your plan? There's only a bloody couple of hundred rotters surrounding us. You've got to have a plan, right? I can't take this. I really can't." Jacob slumped to his knees by the door, tears pouring over his cheeks.

Lori's eyes darted to Elijah. He simply stood above Michael's unconscious form, watching Jacob. "We need another vehicle," he said at last. "The van is broken."

"No. . . really?" Jacob wailed. "I would never have figured that one out!"

"Calm yourself, Jacob," Elijah ordered him. "The city is full of them."

"Yeah, that's wonderful, Elijah. We can't even open the blasted doors without getting overrun. How exactly are you going to get a new one for us?"

Lori saw Elijah staring at Jacob as if he too was wondering if the writer had truly lost it or if this was just a normal breakdown from the stress they were under.

"Jacob," Elijah said, "we can still go up." Elijah pointed at the ceiling.

Jacob buried his face in his hands, his body shaking with sobs.

"Up?" Lori asked.

Elijah nodded. "We can escape from the roof. Everything we need to do so is here. It won't be easy given your husband's current condition but it is possible."

"Tell me more," Lori said.

"I will bring a new vehicle here. We'll create a

diversion as the rest of you get aboard then we'll continue on as planned."

"And if you don't make it back?" Lori asked though she didn't really want to.

"Another of you will try or you'll all die here," Elijah said flatly without a trace of emotion in his voice.

Michael groaned, stirring where he sat. "No, Lori," he begged her.

"No, what, hon?" Lori moved to kneel in front of him, taking his hands in her own. They were cold and clammy on her skin.

"I can see it in your eyes. You're thinking about going with him."

"I'm sorry, Michael, I can't sit by and do nothing. That's not who I am and you know it." Lori gave Michael a quick kiss then turned to Elijah.

"I work better alone," he argued.

"I don't care. Let's get to it."

There was no access to the roof until Elijah made one with a pus covered chainsaw they found. The sky was black and starless as Lori stood beside him now overlooking what remained of the rotters below. "Storm's coming," she commented, feeling the static in the air.

Elijah grunted in response. "There's less than I imagined," he admitted, "Still gonna need to be careful though. A scratch is just as lethal as a bite."

"So?" Lori asked. "Where are we getting our new rig? I mean there's a pickup sitting right over there." She pointed at a red truck in the street a few yards beyond the edge of the morgue's parking lot.

"It's too open," Elijah told her. "On the way in we passed an Outback that looked to be in pretty good shape. It's a block or so North. That's where we'll start."

Elijah removed a compacted crossbow from his coat and began to unfold it. He loaded it with a bolt that was attached to a thin, wire climbing cable. Tying the wire to a metal pipe on the roof, he fired the crossbow. The bolt fell into the asphalt of the lot below, imbedding itself there.

"We slid down and hit it hard and fast. There will be no stopping until we reach the vehicle. Are you sure you want to do this?"

"Totally," Lori stood her ground.

Elijah tossed her a pair of thick gloves. "These worked for Jacob. Put them on."

Lori complied. They were a tad big but she guessed they would serve their purpose.

Before she could say anything else, Elijah took a running leap, grabbing the cable as he plummeted from the roof and slid into the parking lot. He knocked aside several rotters as he reached the ground, drawing twin pistols from underneath his trench coat. His shots echoed in the night as he began to send the closest creatures to Hell where they belonged.

Cursing, Lori grabbed the cable and jumped off the roof. As soon as her feet touched the parking lot, she was running after Elijah through the path his guns had cut in the rotters' ranks. Her UZIs blazed, the bursts from their barrels flashing in the darkness.

"This way," she heard Elijah yell as he kicked in the rear door of the warehouse neighboring the morgue. Lori saw what he planning. By cutting through the warehouse, odds were they would lose the bulk of the rotters on their tail. She sprinted after Elijah. The two of them wove through aisles of crates and large wooden containers until they reached its other side. Elijah came to a halt at a doublewide door looking to lead back onto the street. He glanced at her and she nodded. Without hesitating, Elijah threw the door open. A small pack of eight surprised rotters snarled at them. Lori emptied the clips of her UZIs, sending them sprawling. Elijah darted through the doorway ahead of her. His pistols were holstered, his swords in his hands.

The street was fairly clear of rotters in comparison to the area around the morgue. Lori paused to close the warehouse door. One good thing about rotters was that most of them didn't know what a door knob was.

As she ran on, Lori let one of her UZIs go as she popped the other's spent clip, shoving a fresh mag into it. She could see the Outback they were after up ahead. Elijah sidestepped a rotter who came racing at him as he neared it. One of his swords gutted the creature as the other slashed its spine in two as he passed it. Another rotter dove around the Outback at him. Elijah cut a deep wound into its face where its eyes had been. Lori watched as he flung open the driver side door.

"Cover me!" Elijah shouted, bending under the dash and tearing loose the wires he would need to hotwire it. Lori came to a halt just short of his position. One after another, the rotters who charged them were met with bursts of automatic fire, tearing flesh and spraying stale blood on the street.

The Outback's engine roared to life. Lori didn't wait for an invitation. She ran for its passenger door. A rotter met her as she rounded the rear of the vehicle. She raised her UZI at its snarling lips. Her heart froze as she squeezed the weapon's trigger and it clicked empty. The rotter's hands grabbed her shoulders, slamming her into the Outback's side. Her UZI bounced away as it was knocked from her grasp and fell to the pavement. She struggled against the rotter's hold on her, kneeing it in the groin with no effect. Its teeth snapped at her flesh. Frantically, Lori got her arms up in between the rotter's. She wasn't strong enough to push it off of her so she shoved her thumbs into its eyes, pressing as hard as she could. Its decayed tissues gave way with a sickening, popping noise as her thumbs sank into its sockets. Thick, stale blood oozed over her hands and down her arms but still the thing refused to let go. Glass shattered next to her as a round from one of Elijah's pistols came through the Outback's rear side window and splattered the rotter's torso open in a shower of guts and pus. Lori screamed, a fresh wave of adrenaline pulsing through her, and pushed the off balance rotter from its feet. Several more of the creatures were almost within grabbing distance of her as she hopped into the passenger seat. "Go!" she yelled at Elijah. The Outback peeled out as it lurched forward.

Lori's breathing was hard and fast, her eyes glistening with tears. She noticed Elijah steal a glance at her. "I'm okay," she lied. By the grace of God, the rotter hadn't broken her skin with its teeth or nails but it had shaken her to her very core. With trembling hands, she drew the pistol on her belt and tried to ready it.

"Elijah," Lori asked, "where were you when all this started?" She hoped talking would help her reign in her emotions.

"An army base."

"Wow," Lori tried to smile. "That explains so much. Were you in command there?"

"It was. . .unpleasant," Elijah answered then changed the subject. "Your husband will die from his wound. Do you want to be the one?"

"But he didn't get bit," Lori argued.

"It doesn't matter. The virus has become airborne."

"How could you possibly know that?"

"I can do it if you want," Elijah offered. "You know I'm telling the truth."

Lori forced down her anger. "No, I

"Anger is good," Elijah told her. "It gives you strength. Control it and it may keep you alive but it won't change what will happen to Michael. It's only a matter of time."

Jacob and the others were waiting on the roof when they arrived. Jacob lobbed a belt of grenades over the edge of the roof into the rotters below as the morgue came into view. Elijah reduced the Outback's speed as the explosion shook the parking lot, then he punched it, driving through the flames and rain of splattered body parts as Lori held herself in place in the passenger seat with white knuckled hands. The Outback's brakes squealed, straining to stop the vehicle as Elijah brought it around to the side of the morgue.

Lori and Elijah leapt from the Outback, providing cover fire against the few rotters left standing, as the others made their way down from the roof. Michael looked worse than ever as Jacob helped him into the Outback's hatch. The pieces of lab coat tied as bandages over his stomach were a wet shade of red. His skin was pale and sweaty. Lori was the last person to get in. her final shot making a mess of an elderly lady's gray hair as Lori's bullet cracked her skull. Jacob was smiling at her as Lori turned to look into the backseat. Helena sat next to him, clearly terrified but holding it together.

"Where to now?" Jacob asked.

"Out of the city," Elijah said.

"Good," Lori laughed bitterly. "It's about time we got the Hell out of Dodge."

Michael lay propped against the side of the

Outback in the hatch area behind the backseat. His pain was so intense, his knuckles were white where he clutched the floor as he tried to keep from being sent flying about by Elijah's wild driving. Lori was so far away in the passenger seat, she might as well have been on the moon. There was so much he wanted to say to her but he couldn't, not in front of the others. He grunted through gritted teeth as the Outback hit a pothole and jostled him, causing his muscles to tense up. Michael could feel parts of him hanging out of the open mess of his wound underneath his makeshift bandages. He never imagined he'd go like this or that death would hurt so much. Memories of better days played through his mind like short movies. He remembered when he met Lori. The way she looked all sweaty and out of place on the gym's treadmill that day. The smell of her hair as her head rested on his chest in their bed. How she hated mushrooms and complained every time he cooked them. He thought about the child they had been planning and the future that would never be. Michael promised her he would never hurt her or let her down. He was breaking that promise now and that fact hurt him as much as the shotgun had. A moan escaped his lips.

"You okay back there?" Jacob asked, twisting his head around over the top of the backseat.

"What do you think?" Michael snapped. He hated the nerdy writer mainly because he figured Lori would one day end up in Jacob's arms after he was gone.

"You were kind of scaring me there for a moment," Jacob droned on.

Michael ignored him until Jacob left him alone. Closing his eyes, he rested his head on his chest. Maybe he would get lucky and bite the prick's nose off when he turned, before one of the others put a bullet in his brain. As he fell asleep, Michael dreamed of chewing on Jacob's flesh and tearing it apart with his teeth.

Neither Jacob nor Helena saw it coming when Michael's corpse rose up in the hatch several minutes later and grabbed Jacob's head by handful of his hair, jerking it backwards. Helena screamed louder than Jacob as the writer twisted about, trying to get free of Michael's hold. Helena knew she had to do something, anything. Her hands latched onto the sides of the thing that was once Michael's head. His flesh was feverishly hot against her skin but there was no doubt in her mind that he was dead. She strained, tugging him away from Jacob.

"Michael!" Lori shouted from the front of the vehicle.

"Kill it!" Elijah barked, unable to offer any help.

Helena released Michael as Jacob turned in his seat, wrestling him. Michael tried to force his way over the top of the backseat to flop onto them. Helena reached for Jacob's pistol where he had dropped it into the floorboard. Her fingers closed around it. She'd never held a gun before much less used one. The feel of the weapon in her hand sent a rush of excitement coursing through her. Helena sat up.

"Shoot it! Shoot it!" Jacob was yelling at her. Michael gave a low, guttural moan as his soulless, hungry eyes cut towards her, as if a shred of understanding of what a gun was remained within him.

Helena pressed the pistol's barrel to the side of his head and squeezed the trigger. A spray of bone fragments and brain matter flew over Jacob and the Outback's hatch window as the bullet exited Michael's skull. Michael's body slouched over and slid into the floor of the hatch to lay still. Helena giggled like a little girl at the mess she had made. Jacob stared at her. She realized what she was doing and stopped suddenly. "I. . .I am sorry," she said, handing the gun to Jacob. "I don't know what came over me."

"Don't worry about it. You just saved my life," Jacob said, but Helena barely heard him over the sound of Lori's wailing. Helena reached to put a hand on Lori's shoulder to comfort her but Lori slapped it away.

"Don't you touch me!" Lori's eyes were full of hatred and torment.

"She only did what had to be done," Elijah commented. "You knew this was coming."

Helena, tortured by her own guilt at enjoying what she had done, tried to block out Lori's sobs. Her gaze drifted to the rotters outside the window who were trying to chase them as the Outback sped along the freeway. These people had saved her from

Mark but she didn't know who they were. Not really. The four of them needed to get along and she hoped her action to save Jacob hadn't destroyed the chance of a real friendship with Lori in the days that lay ahead. They might be the only two women left alive on the whole planet. Helena shivered. She could still hear Mark's voice in her ears whispering, "Call me Daddy," as he pumped away between her thighs. The sicko took her virginity. She was glad he was dead. Michael appeared to be a decent and good man though. She could understand Lori's pain but as Elijah said, she'd done the right thing, the thing that had to be done. Was it her fault that she had been the only one who could do it?

Jacob was having about as much success comforting Lori as she had. Finally, he gave up and turned to her, shaking his head. "It wasn't your fault."

"I know," Helena admitted, touching his cheek softy with her fingertips. "It's not yours either."

They drove on in silence, leaving the city behind them.

PART II:
Road Trip

As the sun rose above the fields of green, Thomas walked the perimeter of the farm. The grass was wet with dew, sparkling in the early light. Another time, he might have found it all to be beautiful, but not today. A rotter was caught on the electric fence that ran the length of his property. Smoke rose from its twitching form as its burning flesh popped and crackled.. The air stank of decay and cooking meat. Taking care to make sure he was grounded, Thomas used a long stick to peel the dead man's fingers from the fence. The corpse's brain was fried. Once free, the rotter collapsed on the other side of the fence and lay still. The TV said the cities were gone and the president dead before its screen became a forever dance of black and white snow, the voices of the news reporters replaced with static. Other than their stink, Thomas didn't mind the rotters so much. Here in the middle of nowhere, their numbers were too few to be a real threat unless you got stupid and careless. Thomas almost pitied the creatures. He had known cows smarter than most of these things were. He finished his walk, heading up the hill to his house. The screen door on the front porch was flopping in the gentle morning breeze as he walked up the steps. Thomas stomped the mud from his boots and let himself in. Duke and Hunter met him. He squatted, scratching each of their heads in turn.

"Bet you buys are hungry, huh? Tell you what. I'll fry us up some eggs here in a second, okay?"

Thomas stood, propping his rifle against the kitchen table. The farms always yielded more than he needed to make it. Even before the rotters came, Thomas seldom headed into town. The only two things he was really going to miss when his supplies ran out were cigarettes and coffee. He supposed he could live without the cigarettes if he changed over to smoking a pipe and started growing more tobacco as part of his crop. He always kept a small patch in the garden. It was something his father always did and he carried on the tradition without ever honestly knowing why he did it. It wouldn't be hard to expand. The coffee though. . .that was irreplaceable. Tea just didn't cut it as a substitute. Maybe he was a Yankee, he could deal with tea, but he was a good old southern boy and proud of it. Yep, aside from the coffee issue, he pretty well had it made. So far, the power was even still on. He didn't expect that to last though, but it was nice for the moment. He took a half dozen eggs, a bottle of ketchup, and a jug of milk from the fridge and went to work on making breakfast. The dogs watched him as he cooked. He placed one heaping plate of steaming eggs on the floor for them and took a seat at the table with his own.

As he shoveled a forkful into his mouth, he thought again about trying to hike over to old man Hall's farm to check on him. That codger was too stubborn to die from such a minor problem as hungry, dead people roaming around. If he worked up the courage to go, Thomas was fairly sure he would find the old man working his still like he did everyday. It wasn't that he was afraid of the rotters. It was how the animals in the woods were acting all spooked that bothered him. Who knew what the rotters were driving out of hiding and down from the mountains? Thomas had no desire to come across a displaced and angry Grizzly. There was a half a tank of gas in his Ford but using the truck brought on a whole other set of problems. For one, he'd be exposed on the road. Every dang rotter in earshot would come running as soon as they heard the engine. Worst of all though, even if he made it to old man Hall's and back, was the certainty that the things would follow him home. Odds were there would be too many for him to handle alone, even with the fence, the traps he had set and his guns. The truck was a risk he couldn't take unless he was prepared to possibly abandon his home. Even if he ditched it and walked, there would be no guarantee of not being followed on foot after having drawn as much attention as the truck's engine would. Thomas promised himself he'd figure a way to see the old man yet but he didn't have time to dwell on it any longer this morning. There were chores to be done and they weren't going to tend to themselves.

One of Thomas's current projects was cutting firewood for the coming winter. August wasn't that far from the colder nights of November as he saw it. If he was still breathing then, he would need something to burn. Wood would be his only source for heat and means to cook with because one day soon the power was going to go out and it would never be coming back on. It was work that Thomas hated but his pa didn't raise no slacker.

Carrying his ax and his rifle, Thomas marched through the backdoor and into the yard with Duke and Hunter nipping playfully at his heels. Better to get it done before the day got too hot and the sun was high in the sky. Thomas led the dogs through the gate onto the road. He had been clearing the woods around the property as he gathered his firewood. Two birds, one stone and all that. The dogs followed him as he cut back up the hill, walking beside the fence, to the area he'd been working on.

Bringing the dogs along was sort of a safety net. They hated the dead. If any of the rotters came stumbling through the trees, there was no chance of them sneaking up on him. Duke and Hunter would tip him off to their presence long before they got close enough to be a threat. He worried about the dogs but whatever it was that caused the dead to rise up after the flesh of the living had only affected humans so far. That brought him some comfort and quite frankly he needed them. He wouldn't be able to do this without them.

Thomas picked a tree and went to work. The blade of his ax thudded into it a thick trunk. Wasn't but three swings later that Duke and Hunter suddenly went nuts. Their barking was frantic and loud, unlike anything Thomas expected. He flung his ax to the ground and grabbed his rifle from where it lay in the grass nearby. Sweat trickled down his back as he chambered a round in the .30-.06's chamber. From how the dogs were acting, either a whole horde of rotters was coming or the devil himself was headed down the mountain towards them. A roar so loud it seemed to shake the trees answered the dogs. Hunter and Duke went silent, except for a quiet whimpering, tucking their tales between their legs. Thomas felt like he was being watched. He wanted to run but something inside of him made him stand his ground. Whatever was in the woods sure wasn't a rotter and his life might depend on knowing what it was. Thomas heard the sound of breaking limbs as something larger than a bear and as fast as a car tore through the trees heading to the North, away from his position. He raised his rifle, bracing its butt against his shoulder as he took aim at the area where the movement was. His finger twitched on the trigger but he didn't pull it. Instead, he whirled about and ran for home, calling for the dogs to follow him.

●●●

"Elijah, I really don't think this is a good idea," Jacob said as Elijah steered the Outback up to the pumps of the Mom and Pop gas station. The town they were in was a small one. Jacob thought he remembered seeing a sign that read "Clyde" or something like that. He supposed the place's name didn't matter. Not much did anymore. They'd only seen a handful of rotters staggering its streets so far and those had been pretty scattered. The station's lot was clear of them for now. But that didn't mean there wasn't an army of them somewhere in the buildings or woods nearby.

"It's this or walk," Elijah scowled. "We used the last of what was onboard this morning."

Jacob hoped Lori would take his side but she was still a wreck. She sat in the passenger seat beside Elijah staring at the dashboard. Her eyes were so red it looked almost like they were bleeding. There was a glistening layer of snot between her upper lip and nose. Jacob felt bad for her but there was nothing he could do to help her. The grief she was feeling was too deep, too personal for him to do anything to drag her out of it.

Helena, on the other hand, was really coming alive. She had asked Elijah for a weapon and held onto the .38 revolver he had given her like a Round

Table knight clutching Excalibur.

Elijah threw the Outback into park and killed the engine. "The power's on here. This should be fast and easy."

Jacob stepped from the Outback with him. He needed to stretch his legs. "I'm starving," Jacob complained as he eyed the station; his earlier fear was replaced by the desire to fill his belly.

"Take Helena with you if you go," Elijah ordered him.

Jacob saw Helena perk up even more at her name. Her door swung open on the other side of the vehicle. She walked around to join them at the pumps, beaming and bristling with energy.

"Okay then. We'll be back in a few." Jacob nodded at Elijah, then smiled at Helena. "You sure you know how to use that?"

She held up the revolver in her hands like a model on a Charlie's Angels poster. "Don't worry," she giggled, "I won't shoot you. . .intentionally."

The station's windows were shattered. Shards of glass littered the pavement. "Be careful and watch where you step," Jacob told Helena. She was still barefoot and he didn't want her getting hurt from something as stupid not paying attention and ending up with her feet more injured than they already were.

The door was unlocked. Jacob peeked through its plexi-glass to check for rotters waiting inside before he opened it. A small silver bell jingled above them as they entered. Shredded potato chip bags, stepped-on candy bars, and other trash covered the floor, crunching and crackling underneath their feet.

"Guess this place has been looted before," Jacob commented, a bit disappointed at that fact. The register on the counter was open and all the money gone. He wondered what sort of idiot would take the time to do that. What value could green paper possibly have now?

"Wow. Even most of the condoms are gone," Helena chuckled as she stared into the closest of the three aisles in front of the rear refrigerator section.

"How old are you again?" Jacob teased her.

Helena frowned. "I'm seventeen."

Jacob patted her shoulder as he walked by her into an aisle. "Forget it. I was only messing with you. Help me look around. There has to be something left we can use."

Helena loosed an excited squeal as he lifted a can of baked beans for him to see.

"Well at least that's something," Jacob said.

They spent another five minutes searching the place over before Jacob heard Elijah yell for them. In addition to the beans, they found a few loose bottles of water and a handful of unopened candy bars that made Jacob cringe as he remembered his time locked in his office building's break room. Helena was already chewing on a Snickers as they met Elijah at the Outback. Elijah had pulled it closer to the station once its tank was full. Jacob noticed the bodies of three rotters lying in the parking lot. Elijah was leaning against the Outback's hood, wiping stale blood from the blade of one of his swords with a dirty cloth.

"Company?" Jacob asked. Elijah ignored him. Jacob tossed him a candy bar. Elijah caught it and flung back at him.

"What?" Jacob said. "They didn't have any Oreos, okay? Sorry, mate."

Thomas sat at the kitchen table, a beer in his hand. He replayed the events of the morning over and over in his head. Try as he might, he couldn't come up with any rational explanation for what that. . .thing in the woods could have been. Maybe none of it was real. Maybe being alone was already getting to him. If it weren't for Duke and Hunter, he'd be more than happy to believe he'd imagined it all. The dogs were proof that something had happened, however. They sulked around acting as scared as he was. Thomas gulped down what remained of his beer and crushed the can. He wanted to talk to someone. Old man Hall was the only hope of that. He got up from the table, his heavy boots clomping on the wooden floor as he walked across the kitchen to peer through the window above the sink. It wasn't quite one o'clock yet. If he hustled, he could easily reach old man Hall's farm before sundown. The time for making excuses was over. It was time to man up and just go. Thomas pocketed some extra rounds for his rifle from an open box sitting on the kitchen counter near the door. "See you boys tomorrow," he told the dogs. "Try not to tear the house apart while I'm gone, okay?"

Duke and Hunter whined at him. "You'll be fine," he assured them as he thought *and Lord willing so will I.*

There was no safe path to old man Hall's farm or he would've made this trip days ago when the world started becoming a living Hell. The woods were completely out of the question so he took the road. The heat was blistering as he walked. His .30.-06 was slung over his shoulder by its strap and he carried a shovel in his hands. Shovels were surprisingly effective weapons against the rotters. Its edges could chop into a decaying head rather easily and the length of its handle helped as well. Thomas kicked a rock, sending it bouncing along the asphalt ahead of him. His eyes darted from one side of the road to the other. Being so exposed like this would have made him nervous even without the events of the morning. His shovel offered no protection against the thing he'd encountered. He wondered if his rifle would. As fast as the thing appeared to be, he might not be able to get off a shot if it came barreling from the woods at him. There was no certainty a single shot would stop something that large in its tracks either. Deciding he was spooked enough, he tried not to think about the beast or whatever it was, turning his mind instead to old man Hall. If the stubborn old man was still alive as Thomas suspected, what then? Would he offer him a place at his farm? He doubted very much Hall would even consider such an offer but they'd both be a lot safer with someone else around. The old man would likely trade with him though if he could bring himself to make this trip again after today. That alone was worth the journey. Hall's moonshine was famous all around these parts. Having some for medicinal purposes would be a good thing. Exchanging seeds with the old man would broaden both of their crops as well. Thomas hoped Hall would be in a good mood when he got there. Some of Hall's shine would make it a lot easier to talk to the old man about what he had seen.

The sun was sinking behind the mountains as Thomas reached the winding, gravel road leading up to old man Hall's farm. The old man rarely used it so it was in pretty rough shape. It wasn't exactly wide to being with and the encroaching vegetation made it even narrower. The long shadows of the early fall twilight added to its creepiness. Thomas stuck his shovel in the dirt, unslinging his rifle. Better to be safe than sorry, he told himself, making sure the gun had a round ready to go in its chamber. Thomas trudged along the drive half expecting old man Hall to pop out in front of him with a shotgun and accidentally blow his face off.

"Mr. Hall!" he shouted as he neared the farm. "You around here?"

Last Stand In A Dead Land

Thomas could see the house ahead. There were no lights on in it. That didn't mean anything of course. The power could have finally died during his walk and it wasn't quite totally dark yet either. To the house's right was the huge pasture where the old man kept his livestock. Thomas froze as he saw the dead cattle scattered across the field. Part of the fence was smashed and knocked over as if something huge had crashed right through it. Thomas's grip on his rifle grew tighter. Several of the cattle appeared to be gutted. One was missing its head. The wind changed and the smell now hit him. Thomas gagged, raising a hand to his mouth as he tried not to vomit. Trails of bent, red-smeared grass told him whatever had killed them had dragged some of them off afterwards. Tearing his eyes away from the massacre in the pasture, Thomas made a run for the house, his legs pumping beneath him as his breath came in ragged gasps of terror. "Mr. Hall!" Thomas screamed as he hurled himself up the steps leading to the front door. One of the steps gave way under his heavy boots with the splintering sound of busting wood. Thomas screamed again, this time a pain-filled wail, as shards of the broken wood scraped at and buried themselves in his leg. His chin smacked into the porch as he fell forward, cutting his cry short. His teeth closed together on the edge of his tongue. Thomas spat out a mouthful of blood. He rolled over where he lay, searching for his rifle. The impact of his fall had sent it flying from his hands. He thanked God as he saw it was

70

within reach and grabbed it. There was still no sign of old man Hall. Lifting his leg, Thomas grimaced both from the pain of the movement and what he saw. His pants leg was torn and wet with blood that continued to pour from a long gash stretching from just above the top of his boot all the way to his knee. It took all Thomas had not to pass out in that moment. Gritting his teeth against the pain, he crawled onto the porch. The partially cracked front door creaked on its hinges, making him jump. The light was fading quickly now as night closed in. Thomas noticed something lying on the living room floor. He squinted, trying to make out what it was. Deciding he didn't care, he dragged himself on into the house, kicking the door shut behind him with his good leg. The whole room was spinning as his strength gave out and the darkness claimed him.

Lori felt better. No, that was a lie, she admitted to herself. She felt like an eighteen wheeler ran over her and smeared the mangled mess of her body along the interstate as it kept going. But she was alive, whatever that was worth. She didn't remember burying Michael. The memory of her pulling her pistol on Elijah and demanding that they do it was, however, very clear in her mind. Elijah sat in the driver's seat with the same cold, hard expression he always wore. A drizzle of rain splashed on the windshield of the Outback as it worked its way through the mess of other abandoned cars that littered the road. When folks had fled the town, when the plague started, they must have all headed in this direction.

It was eerie how dark it was. The Outback's headlights were the only source of light on the road. She craned her neck to look into the backseat. Jacob and Helena were asleep. The young girl was cuddled close to Jacob with her head resting on his chest. So much of this day and the night before were lost to a fog of tears, heartbreak, and pain. She wondered when the two of them had gotten so cozy. A pang of jealousy she couldn't explain stung her.

"You hungry?" Elijah asked.

Lori jerked her gaze around to him, feeling guilty. "How long have I. . .?"

"There's a candy bar and bottle of water in the glove box for you," Elijah said.

"Thank you." Lori ripped the wrapper from the candy bar and tore into it, wolfing it down in only a couple of bites.

"Easy," Elijah warned. "You've been through a lot."

"We all have," Lori agreed. She sipped at her water. "Helena seems to be doing better," she said before she could stop herself, hoping Elijah didn't catch the bitterness in her tone.

"She is," he nodded.

Lori was at a loss as to what else to say but she wanted to talk. She couldn't handle the silence right now. "Where are we?" she asked.

"There's a farm not far from here. I stayed there for a while many, many years ago. It should be safe."

"That's not exactly what I asked?"

Elijah shrugged.

"We there yet?" Lori heard Jacob ask from the backseat. She saw his eyes go wide as she turned to look at him.

"Lori," he grinned, "welcome back to the land of the living."

Helena stared at her too. The girl was on the verge of tears as she said, "I'm so sorry, Lori."

Lori shook her head. "Don't go there." She knew Michael's death wasn't Helena's fault but she didn't trust her emotions yet. The girl had lived through enough already without her losing control and adding to the mess.

"We're going to a farm," Jacob told her. Lori caught the frustration and sarcasm in the words.

"So I've heard," she shifted in her seat. "Elijah how do you even know the place you remember is still there?"

"Call it a hunch."

"We're risking a lot on your hunch."

"No more than you've risked before."

Lori managed not to punch his teeth in somehow. "For once can you stop being so vague and just talk like a normal person?"

"I trust him," Helena said out of the blue.

Lori sighed. "That's not the point. We're all equals in this. We should have a say in the plan."

"Something's not right," Elijah told them, ending the argument.

Caught off guard, her train of thought derailed by Elijah's abrupt statement, Lori snapped, "What?"

A roar that shook the night came from somewhere in the woods to the Outback's right. Something huge burst from the trees, smashing into the side of the Outback. The next thing Lori knew, they were flying. The world moved in slow motion as the vehicle flipped over onto its top. She heard voices screaming and realized one of them was her own. Lori's ribs met the dash as she was tossed into Elijah. Her elbow bashed against the steering wheel as she landed below him, in his lap. Elijah was held in place by his seatbelt. Jacob and Helena caught it even worse than she did. They were flung about the rear of the Outback like pinballs.

"Out of my way," Elijah growled at Lori as he popped his seatbelt, shoving her away, and crawled out the driver's side window onto the road. Lori righted herself as she scurried in the opposite direction, the roof now under her knees.

Helena lay across Jacob. The two of them bloody, a mess of jumbled limbs on the Outback's ceiling. They both looked to be breathing. Most of the windows had shattered from the impact.. Lori heard Elijah's pistols firing out on the road, a rapid series of cracking shots. Another roar, half human, half beast, echoed in the darkness outside the car. She screamed again as Elijah's head unrepentantly popped back through the broken window on his side.

"Get them up and moving!" he shouted into her face.

Lori scrambled from the Outback over the broken window glass. She felt it slicing and digging into her hands. Ignoring the pain, she hauled herself out, getting to her feet next to the overturned vehicle. Lori rubbed the glass from her palms and drew her pistol. She jerked her head around as Elijah emptied his own guns at the trees in the distance. Her eyes caught a glimpse of a massive hairy back as something disappeared into the shadows of the woods.

"Where are the others?" Elijah demanded.

Lori couldn't believe it but she saw fear in him. "They're. . .they're unconscious."

"Damn it! Get them! We'll drag them if we have to."

"What was that thing?" Lori asked but Elijah was busy tugging Helena from the wreck, seeing that she was too startled do it, his hands under the girl's arms. Elijah dropped Helena, diving in again for Jacob. As he yanked the nerdy writer onto the road, Jacob stirred.

"Can you move?" Elijah barked at the writer..

"I think so," Jacob said.

Elijah hefted Helena in his arms, carrying her as he ran. Jacob was still shaking his head and trying to clear it as Lori jerked him to his feet. She knew she was going to have to help him. Tossing one of his arms over her shoulders, she dragged him along after Elijah.

Elijah wasn't waiting on them. He moved like a cheetah on speed, unhindered by Helena's weight in his arms.

"Elijah!" Lori yelled at him, knowing she couldn't keep up with Jacob slowing her down. He stopped, waiting on them to reach him, anger seeping out of him.

"The farm is just over the next hill," he told them. "We make it there or die! Do you understand?"

Lori nodded. Jacob was standing on his own now, recovering more with each passing second. A deep, guttural growl came from somewhere behind them.

"What the. . .?" Jacob squealed.

"Run!" Elijah shouted, and they were all moving again as fast as their legs would carry them.

Thomas awoke in darkness. At first he wondered if he was dead but the pain in his leg quickly told him he was alive and totally FUBAR'd. It took him a moment to remember where he was and how he got there. There was a small flashlight in his pocket and he twisted about on the floor as his fingers fished for it. As he sat up, one of his hands brushed against something wet and cold on the floor around him. He clicked on the flashlight to see a sheen of black pus coating the floor. Something was thumping about deeper in the living room. Thomas raised the flashlight, its beam shining onto old man Hall's snarling face. Thomas lurched backwards in an attempt to put as much distance as he could between himself and the old man before he noticed that Hall wasn't getting any closer. The old man's face was a torn mess of shredded flesh. Five, deep, claw-like wounds ran from the top of his forehead to his neck. His jaw was barely attached on one side, swaying awkwardly, as the old man's teeth chomped together over and over again as if he were already chewing on Thomas' skin. One of his arms and the whole lower half of his body were merely gone. His intestines trailed behind him and had gotten wrapped around the leg of the large, handcrafted table in the middle of the room, holding him in a place like chains. Hall's one arm clawed at the air, trying to get at him but Thomas was well far of the old man's reach. Thomas carefully got to his feet, avoiding putting any weight on his injured leg. Only the grace of God had saved him from being rotter food while he was unconscious. Hall's teeth continued to snap vainly as he looked up at Thomas.

Not wanting to waste a bullet, Thomas caved in the old man's skull with the butt of his rifle. Thomas limped by the corpse, turning on a light. The top of the doorway leading into the kitchen was shattered, as if something huge had forced its shoulders though it. He could see pieces of the house's backdoor covering the kitchen floor from where it must have exploded inward as something large had entered. The old man's missing arm lay next to the sink like it had been flung there and forgotten. The ceiling was damaged too. Thomas knew this was the work of the beast he had encountered in the woods. There were footprints in the blood and pus slicking the floor. They looked very much like a barefoot human's would except for their size. The prints were massive, several times the size of his own feet. A single word tumbled through his mind: Bigfoot. Leaning up against the broken doorway of the kitchen, Thomas caught his breath, trying hard to figure out what to do. Start with the leg, a rational voice from somewhere within him said, but all he wanted to do was run.

Thomas hobbled to the old man's bathroom, tearing through the contents of its medicine cabinet until he found a bottle of rubbing alcohol. He poured the entire bottle over the wounds on his leg and nearly blacked out. When the pain subsided, he found some bandages in the mess he had made and plopped onto the toilet to wrap his leg. He was in no shape to try to get home but he wasn't staying here. That much he knew for sure. He rather would deal with a horde of rotters than come face to face with the beast that had ripped its way in here and killed old man Hall. Exhausted and hurting, Thomas staggered from the house as the sun peeked over the tops of the distant mountains.

Old man Hall's ancient and rusted truck sat

parked behind the house. Thomas sank into its driver's seat, happy to be off his feet again. He didn't know squat about hotwiring a vehicle but he was going to have to learn and fast. He tore loose some wires from the steering wheel and hoped they were the correct ones. Five minutes later, after twisting various wires together and crossing his fingers, the truck's engine turned over and came to life. The fuel gauge registered a bit under half a tank but that was more than he needed to get home. As he slammed the truck's door, two rotters rounded the corner of the house, loping like marionettes with broken strings. When the things saw him they came rushing towards the truck, the smell of his flesh and warm blood driving them wild. Cursing, Thomas threw the pickup into drive and floored the gas. The old truck wasn't fast enough. The quicker of the two rotters grabbed the open passenger side window and lunged into the cab with him. He slammed the truck into park and met it with a punch to its nose. Bone crunched beneath his knuckles. Thomas grabbed the thing by its hair, slamming its head against the dashboard. The rotter bared its teeth at him as it broke loose of his hold. Thomas unsheathed the bowie knife strapped to his the side of his right boot and drove it up into the soft flesh of the rotter's chin. The tip of the blade protruded from the rotter's hair for a fleeting second before Thomas put a hand on the thing's forehead and yanked the blade free. Cold hands closed on his shoulders from behind. The other rotter had rounded the truck and was trying to pull him out through the driver's side window. Thomas felt its dirty fingernails drag over the cloth of his shirt as he jerked away from it. He gunned the gas blindly. The truck leapt forward, sending the rotter flailing backwards as the truck left it behind. Thomas sat up, grabbing the wheel just in time to avoid crashing into the fence surrounding the pasture. Cutting the wheel hard, Thomas spun the truck to the side, bouncing along the narrow drive towards the road.

Jacob saw Elijah draw his swords as the rotters sprinted along the road at them. The things had come out of nowhere. They numbered a good dozen or more. Their hungry cries rose in pitch as they drew closer. Jacob didn't have a clue how many bullets remained in his pistol's clip. He just started shooting. His first shot caught a rotter in its shoulder, spraying brown, tainted blood, but did little else. The rotter didn't even slow down. Lori's hand must have been steadier because the rotter she aimed at did a half spin as her bullet blew a gaping hole in the gray flesh below its hairline. Helena froze. Jacob moved between her and the rotters as he tried for another shot and his pistol clicked empty. He cursed and fished in his pockets in a desperate attempt to find another clip. As he did so, Lori dropped two more of the creatures. Elijah sprang forward to meet the other rotters. He dove into their ranks, his swords slashing and hacking as fast as the beat of a hummingbird's wings. Jacob watched in awe as Elijah took the heads off two of the creatures in a single fluid movement, then spun to slice the spine of a third with his left blade while his right plunged into another's skull. Before the rotters' bodies even touched the road, Elijah engaged two more. His right blade flashed, splitting a rotter's face up its middle. Brain matter flew into the air above its scalp as the blade exited the top of its head. His left blade claimed the other rotter's hand as it reached for him. Elijah stepped closer to the rotter, knocking it over. His swords spun above his head, twirling on his fingers, then met inside the rotter's skull as they descended into the creature's eyes. For all Elijah's speed, the rotters were just too many. As Elijah rose to meet the next wave, a dead man in a football uniform plowed into him, taking him to the ground. As Elijah struggled with the dead man, the remaining two charged at Jacob. He kept Helena behind him and shoved Lori from their path.

Jacob met the first rotter, a dead woman in a torn blouse and blood-stained skirt, head on. His fist collided with her jaw, breaking it along with one of his knuckles. Jacob yelped, shaking his hand from the pain, as the woman staggered sideways. The second rotter, a heavily decayed older man in farmer's overalls, scratched at the sleeve of his shirt. Jacob screamed as the farmer's other hand closed around his throat. A dull thunk took Jacob by surprise. He felt the farmer's grip go limp around his neck and the rotter fell forward into Jacob's arms. One of Elijah's throwing knives was buried in the backside of its skull. The farmer's weight was too much for him. Jacob flopped to the ground with the rotter's corpse on top of him. Jacob screamed louder, rolling the farmer off of him.

"You idiot!" Lori yelled. "What were you thinking?"

"What?" Jacob shouted, scrambling to his feet, rubbing his swollen fist. "I just saved your bloody life!"

He noticed Elijah walking over to them as they argued. The man was soaked in red, brown, and black goo. Before any of them could say anything more, a fresh chorus of snarls and howls erupted from the trees around them. He watched Elijah shift into a defensive posture, his blades ready for whatever was coming. An inhuman cry arose in the trees, followed by the sounds of battle.

"Yeah!" Jacob yelled, jumping like a giddy schoolgirl. "Get 'em!"

"I wouldn't be too happy," Elijah pointed out. "When it's done with the rotters, we're next on the menu."

"Shut up!" Lori told them both. "Do you hear that?"

Jacob listened closely. Something was coming up the road. A rusty and ancient looking Ford truck sped around the bend, angled straight for them. The driver must have seen them because the truck's brakes squealed, trying to stop it. Its momentum was so great that the vehicle spun sideways across the road as it came to a stop. A tired, redneck man sat in the driver's seat staring at them with his mouth hanging open in pure shock.

"Who the Hell are you?" Jacob asked.

"Guess right now, I'm the guy saving your butts," the redneck laughed, "but you can call me Thomas."

A gnawed-upon arm came flying from the woods to land near the truck as the night fell quiet once more.

"I suggest you folks hop in. I ain't staying around to find out what's going on here. I gotta feeling, I don't want to know."

Thomas was already turning the truck as Elijah, Lori, and Helena leapt into its bed. Jacob slid into the passenger seat. He noticed Thomas's leg. "You okay, man?"

"I'll live, I reckon," Thomas answered.

"Go!" Jacob heard Elijah yell from the back of the truck as a massive beast came lumbering onto the road behind them.

"What is that thing?" Jacob muttered as it punched a tree, cracking its trunk.

"Bigfoot," Thomas told him. "It's freaking Bigfoot."

The truck sped along the road, its speed increasing as it went. The beast was chasing after them. It moved impossibly fast for something so large. Its yellow eyes burned with a fury unlike Elijah had ever seen in a living creature before. He knew the beast was called Bigfoot, Sasquatch, or any of a dozen other names. Elijah cursed, pounding the side of the pickup's bed with his fist. He figured he had thought of everything but he had never imagined that such a beast actually existed on this Earth. All of his efforts to get here, all his well laid plans, were threatened by a monster that shouldn't be real but was. Lori and Helena were straining to hold on and not be flung from the truck's bed as the redneck driving tried to keep them ahead of it. The backwoods road they were on was narrow and winding, allowing the beast to stay on their tail. Elijah placed its speed at near forty miles an hour. He couldn't chance it catching up with them.

Elijah stood up in the center of the truck's bed, balancing himself like a surfer riding a wave. Drawing his pistols form the holsters underneath his trench coat, he started popping off shots at the monster. Even with his level of skill, the motion of the truck made it hard to score a decent hit. For every round that struck the beast, another went wild or buried itself in a tree. The bullets that did manage to hit the beast had little effect. At best, they produced tiny splatters of red in its hair and only seemed to make it angrier from what Elijah could tell. The thing's muscle density was so thick that he wasn't getting any real penetration. He needed a bigger gun, a lot bigger gun. The idea of leaping from the back of the moving truck to the road and facing it with his swords crossed his mind but he was so close to his goal, he couldn't bring himself to chance it. He holstered his pistols, digging around in the pockets of his trench coat. Somewhere in them was a grenade he had swiped as he left the army base when the rotter plague began. Finally, he found it. Yanking its pin, he stared into the beast's yellow eyes as it poured on a fresh burst of speed, bringing it closer to the truck. Elijah threw the grenade at its feet. A flash of fire and shrapnel filled the road behind the truck as he heard Lori and Helena screaming. Whether it was the shockwave from the blast, or loss of focus on his balance, he didn't know, but he lost his footing and slammed hard, face first, into the truck's bed as he fell. He barely had time to jerk an arm between his face and the metal of the bed before he smashed into it. He could still hear Lori's and Helena's horrified cries as his world went black and he lost consciousness.

The explosion in the rearview caused Thomas to swerve too hard as he rounded another bend in the road. The truck's wheels whined in protest as the vehicle slid sideways again. Thomas almost lost control of the truck as it threatened to flip over and go rolling into the bank that ran along the side of the road. He righted the truck, struggling against the jerking wheel, keeping it moving forward.

"Dude, this isn't a bloody episode of The Dukes of Hazard!" Jacob shouted in his ear.

Thomas checked the rearview to make sure the girls and the weird guy were still in the back of the truck. Seeing that they were okay, Thomas cracked a smile at Jacob. "Can't say we good old boys don't know how to drive."

There was no sign of the beast. Whether it was dead, lying in the road somewhere behind them bleeding, or just gone was anyone's guess. Thomas hoped the weirdo had killed it, but he didn't figure they were that lucky.

"Where are we headed?" Jacob asked him.

Thomas kept his eyes on the road ahead. He didn't' want any more surprises sneaking up on them. "Home," he said after a couple of seconds. "We're going home."

Thomas led the group onto his farm. They had left the truck at the end of the drive heading up to the farm. Thomas turned on the electric fence as they entered through the gate. He doubted it would even slow down the beast if it was still alive and out there in the woods somewhere but it would sure mess up any rotters who had followed them home. At least it would until the creatures' numbers over-loaded it and shorted it out.

Jacob and Lori were dragging Elijah with them, his arms over their shoulders and his weight divided between them. Helena brought up the rear, her .38 revolver held tightly and ready in her trembling hands.

"Nice place you got here," Jacob commented as they reached the front porch of the house.

"I get by," Thomas grinned. "Can't say it's been easy."

Lori laughed darkly, "You're kidding right? You been to the city recently?"

Thomas suddenly felt bad about his choice of words and flippant attitude as he realized what they must have lived through to get here. "Sorry, ma'am. Guess I've taken for granted what I have been blessed with way out here in the backwoods."

"Is that. . ." Jacob pointed to a small building in the distance beyond the house where chickens were pecking at the dirt.

"Yep. It's a hen house. Got some cows too in a pasture over the hill if that dang beast ain't killed them," Thomas bragged.

"Do you have horses?" Helena asked.

Thomas shook his head as he watched disappointment fill her eyes. "Never had need for them, I reckon. Wish I did though. They would come in mighty handy these days."

"The fence is a nice touch," Lori told him, clearly impressed.

"Thank you. It's kept the rotters out so far. Got some bear traps and other nasty things set up too but the fence is my mainline of defense."

"I hate to interrupt," Jacob said, "but can we get somewhere we can put Elijah down. The freak is heavier than he looks."

"Just put him over there." Thomas pointed to a swinging bench at the far side of the porch. Jacob and Lori gently laid Elijah on it.

"He okay?" Thomas asked, knowing that if the man wasn't, there wasn't exactly a whole lot they would be able to do for him. All he owned was a single, very basic first aid kit. Unless one of these folks was a doctor, the poor guy was out of luck if he didn't pull through on his own.

"He's the toughest bugger I have ever met," Jacob said, "I'm sure he's fine."

"I can't believe he was carrying a grenade in his pocket," Thomas admitted.

Lori just grinned. "Hey, it's Elijah."

Thomas didn't know them that well but he got the point of what she said.

Lori looked down at Elijah on the bench. "He took a rather nasty fall when that thing went off. Don't think there's anything we can do though but wait for him to wake up."

"Well then. . ." Thomas smiled so wide it threatened to swallow his face. "You folks look like you could use some food. . . And I know y'all could use a shower." He waved his hand playfully in front of his nose.

"Did you say shower?" Lori asked.

Thomas nodded as she beamed like a supernova of excitement and happiness.

He showed the girls to his bathroom and gave them the towels they would need, cautioning them about the limited supply of hot water due to the small size of the water heater in the cellar. He also left them some clothes, faded jeans and t-shirts, where his washing machine was. As he walked into the kitchen, he could still hear them arguing over who got to go first. Thomas decided having other living people in his home was worthy of good old fashion splurge from his stockpile of supplies. There was some steak and bacon set aside in the freezer. He carried them both to the stove and went to work preparing dinner. He couldn't help but wonder if the girls were spoken for. It had been a long, long time since he'd been with a woman. That Helena was cute as button in a nubile, sexy kind of way. She was as Italian as he was Southern. Her hair was as dark as midnight and her figure. . .oh, man. He hoped his drool hadn't been obvious every time he looked at her. She was a good bit younger than him, obviously still a teenager, but who was to say stuff like that even mattered anymore? She spoke with an air of maturity; likely she'd grown up a lot in the last few days. Surely it had to be a whole new ballgame now if the human race wanted to survive, what with the rotters and so few folks still breathing. As with everything else, you made do with what was available and he . . . he was certainly available if she was.

Having four extra mouths to feed would be a hardship but the extra help the new folks would provide should balance things some. If that beast was dead, heck fire, they could handle the rotters. A trip into town for supplies might be a good idea if they were careful. Batteries, ammo, canned goods, a stop at a pharmacy to upgrade his first aid kit, some more gas for the generator—because they would want it when the power finally did go out as it surely would—and of course coffee were some of the possibilities that crossed his mind.

As the heavenly smell of frying bacon drifted through the kitchen, Thomas realized with a start that Duke and Hunter were missing. It wasn't unlike the dogs to let themselves out the backdoor. There were no signs of trouble in or around that house that he saw. Probably out chasing rabbits and doing their business. He figured they'd come back when they were ready. And if they weren't back by in the morning, he would go hunting for them. His new guests took priority at the moment.

Lori actually shook from pleasure as the hot water exploded from the showerhead and washed over her naked skin. She scrubbed at the dirt, dried blood, and general crud caked onto her skin. Helena sat on the toilet, with the lid down, using it as a chair while she waited on her turn. Lori ran her fingers through her hair and let it flop wetly onto her naked shoulders.

"Lori?" she heard Helena call her name.

"What?" she moaned in response.

"Are we gonna live here? I mean is this our new home?"

"I really hope so kiddo," Lori answered. Something in Helena's voice told her the girl wanted to ask a completely different question. "Thomas is nice but he's too Brad Pitt for me."

"Really?"

"Really. Have at him kiddo. He's all yours," Lori chuckled, but inside she was still mourning Michael and certainly wasn't ready for any new romance.

"Lori?" Helena started again. "Do you think that thing is dead?"

"Don't know. Elijah usually gets the job done but that Bigfoot or whatever it was scared the crap out of him too. Everything was happening so fast, I couldn't do anything but try to hold on and stay in the truck," Lori admitted.

"Me too, but a grenade like that should've killed it don't you think?"

"Everything is gonna be fine, Helena," Lori assured the girl. "Besides," she said, stepping from the shower, a light steam dancing from her body. She didn't want to get out but she knew she had to share. "It's your turn. Come on. Stop worrying so much and let yourself live a little. We're never going to have it this good again."

Helena sprang to her feet, shedding her filthy lab coat and under garments, as Lori watched her with a smile on her face.

As Helena climbed into the shower, Lori shuffled through the stack of clothes Thomas was thoughtful enough to leave in the bathroom beside the towels. They were all men's T-shirts and jeans but Lori didn't care if she looked ridiculous. The shirt she picked was clean and soft on her skin as she slid it over her head. She wiped the condensation from the medicine cabinet's mirror with her bare hand and took a good long look at her reflection. She honestly felt alive again, not just surviving but alive. She sniffed the air. Dear goodness, was that bacon she smelled? Her stomach rumbled a loud and clean affirmative. Lori wondered if she had died on the road when the grenade detonated and if this farm really was heaven.

PART III:
Revelations
and Endings

Jacob sat on the bench next to Elijah. Elijah was a mess. Had it been anyone else, Jacob was sure they would have at least tried to clean them up while they were out. Elijah was a mystery though and gave every impression that he wanted to stay that way. Besides, he wasn't the sort of chap you wanted angry at you. His trench coat was ripped and torn in numerous places and the gore from all their battles crusted onto it. Elijah's wild hair above his goggles reminded Jacob of some Eighties rock singer. He couldn't remember the singer's name but he did remember the song and the video. It was called "Blinded me with Science" or something like that. Elijah would have fit in a steam punk convention pretty well with his weird style. Jacob owed the man his life. As he stared at Elijah, wanting to help him, he noticed one of the lenses of the man's goggles was cracked. Tiny fractures ran across the right lens.

Jacob leaned closer for a better look at the damage. As he did so he noticed small shards of glass imbedded in Elijah's skin below the broken lens. He reached over, trying to rub the glass away with his thumb. Something like blood oozed from around the cuts. Jacob withdrew his hand. Whatever it was, the fluid was a bright greenish yellow, like antifreeze. Jacob didn't really know anything about cars but that was what it made him think of. The writer's breath exploded from him as if someone had punched him in the gut.

Was Elijah infected with the rotter virus? Was he sick? Was that the reason he was so secretive?

Jacob scooted to the other side of the swinging bench without taking his eyes off Elijah. Should he tell the others? What would Elijah do to him when he woke up if he did? If Elijah was infected, Jacob certainly didn't want to be sitting here when he turned. As he thought about what to do, he rubbed a hand through his hair. A low growling drew his attention to the bottom of the steps leading to the porch. Two big, angry dogs sat on their haunches, baring their teeth, between quivering lips, focused on Elijah. Where in the Hades had the things come from? he wondered. Dogs terrified him, always had since he was a boy and one tried to maul him in the park. His dad had saved him that day but the fear had never gone away.

"Thomas!" Jacob shouted into the house. The dogs made no move to attack as he got to his feet and moved slowly, closer to the screen door. The dogs' attention remained centered on Elijah, like they didn't even care that Jacob was there. "Thomas!" Jacob shouted again, banging on the door. "Get out here, man!"

Thomas appeared on the other side of the screen. He looked as if he was about to ask what was going on, then Jacob saw him notice the dogs.

"Duke! Hunter! Down boys!" Thomas yelled at the dogs. If they paid him any attention, Jacob couldn't tell it. Thomas came on out of the house and walked down the steps to them. They relaxed some as he squatted in front of them. "These folks are our guests. Be nice okay?" Thomas ruffled the hair atop their heads, scratched around their ears. "Jacob, I think you'd best take Elijah on in the house. I've never seen them act like this before."

Jacob nodded. "Sure thing." He'd take any excuse to get away from the dogs. Even if it wasn't his blood they seemed to want, they were still creeping him out big time. Jacob propped open the screen door with a chair until he could haul Elijah awkwardly inside to the living room couch. Thomas stayed with the dogs for another few minutes before he followed Jacob inside and shut the heavy interior door behind him.

"I'm sorry," Thomas apologized, shaking his head. "I don't know what's gotten into them."

"No worries, mate," Jacob said, "Hey, is that bacon I smell?"

Thomas smiled. "You bet it is. You ready for some dinner?"

The girls joined them at the table in the kitchen. It was almost surreal for Thomas to be serving guests. The scene was a strange, beautiful, and funny one to him. Lori was the last to take a seat. Thomas knew she had paused to check on Elijah one more time. He was still unconscious on the couch with no signs of waking up anytime soon. Thomas figured Elijah was okay though. He looked to be one tough bastard despite his crazy get up. Anyway, this evening was a celebration of new friendships and the future that lay ahead. There were happier things to dwell on. The sight of Lori in one of his Carolina Panther shirts, several times too large for her, and sagging jeans held in place by a tightly drawn belt around her waist nearly made him laugh. The only piece of her original clothing she still wore were her shoes. Helena stirred a totally different feeling in him. Her feet were still bare, except for the bandages binding them, a fact that he felt very bad about but he didn't have any shoes or boots even close to her size in the house. He'd offered her socks but she'd refused them, choosing to let the wounds on her feet breathe. His mom had passed on a decade ago and after his father's death, Thomas had finally let the last of her belongings go, giving them away to the local Christian Ministries. It was something he regretted now as he saw Helena's poor and bruised feet beneath the table. But what really moved him was that, unlike Lori, the girl wore no pants, only an oversized shirt. The tanned and toned flesh of her thighs peaked at him from below the end of the shirt she wore and it was indeed a fine thing to look at. Both the girls were like different people than the ones who'd entered his bathroom to get cleaned up. Heck, everything was different. Hope had returned to all their lives.

The table was packed with food. There was a steak for each of them, as well as one set aside for Elijah, a plate of crisp bacon, a stack of buttered, store bought dinner rolls Thomas had thawed and warmed up, a heaping bowl of corn, salads made from fresh tomatoes, lettuce, and onions with a healthy splash of ranch dressing, steamed carrots, and two huge pitchers of iced tea so sweet it would rot your teeth just by looking at it.

"I can't believe all this is real," Jacob said, reaching for a roll.

"Wait a second there, speedy," Thomas cautioned him. "Here in the South, we say Grace before we eat."

Thomas bowed his head. "Lord, thank you for this food. Thank you for bringing us all together in this house. Please be with us in the days ahead and show us the way. Your will be done on Earth as it is in Heaven. Amen." ·

As Thomas raised his head, he saw Jacob was staring at him, Lori was smiling, and Helena was weeping with tears of happiness. "I know I ain't much when it comes to saying prayers out loud but. . ."

"You did fine," Lori assured him.

"It was beautiful, Thomas," Helena wiped away her tears. "It was the perfect prayer to begin this perfect meal you've cooked for us with."

Thomas felt his cheeks turning red. "I'm glad to have you all here. I mean that."

"I don't get how you can still believe in God," Jacob said, disgusted.

"Hey," Thomas said, "Not matter how screwed up the world gets, he's still up there watching over us."

Jacob grunted. "Sure, whatever man."

The food disappeared quickly as Thomas's guests gorged themselves, savoring every bite.

"Where did you learn to cook?" Lori asked around a cheekful of salad.

"My parents taught me. Since they died, I have spent most of my life alone so I reckon it's a good skill to have." Thomas poured his second glass of tea and sipped it as they talked.

He noticed Jacob kept stealing glances through the kitchen door at Elijah where he lay sprawled on the couch. "Your friend in there is sure one strange fellow," Thomas commented.

Lori spat a mouthful of tomato into the air. "I'll say!" she laughed. "Wait until you try to have a conversation with him."

Helena frowned at Lori. "Have some respect," the girl said.

Thomas knew to keep his mouth closed. It wasn't his place to say anything. He didn't know any of them that well yet, though he hoped to.

"I'm only speaking the truth," Lori argued.

"Uh, guys," Jacob interrupted. "About Elijah, I think there's something you should know. I think he might be infected."

Thomas clenched his fists, his nails digging into the flesh of his palms as he fought to control his anger. Had these folks brought a rotter into his home? He wanted to jump to his feet, throw over the table, and pummel them all but he kept his cool, if only barely. He hated the question he had to ask. "Was he bitten or scratched?"

A bite spread the virus into a person's blood stream a lot faster than a scratch did. People who were bitten usually turned in a matter of seconds, minutes tops. People who were scratched, that was something he'd never heard much about or experienced, but he knew from the final shreds of news he had heard before the stations went off the air that those folks would turn too. It was only a matter of time.

"Jacob! Why would you even say something like that?" Lori smacked his shoulder so hard Jacob nearly toppled over out of his chair.

"Elijah fell, that's all," Helena added, as if trying to comfort herself.

"I may be crazy," Jacob admitted, "But I think there's something wrong with him, okay? His blood . . ." Jacob cringed as he said the words, "It's yellow."

Thomas let it all sink in as Helena voiced what he was thinking for him, "Rotters don't have yellow blood! Mark did as many terrible things to dozens of them as he did to me. Trust me on this. I never saw yellow blood."

"Who's Mark?" Jacob asked.

Thomas watched Helena turn towards Jacob with an expression so violent he pitied the nerdy writer.

"Oh. . ." Jacob said, his voice going quieter, "I'm sorry."

"Regardless, I think we had better have a closer look at your friend," Thomas said.

Jacob led the group into the living room. Darkness was falling outside so Thomas flicked on the lights as they entered. He stayed in the doorway. There was a pistol in the drawer of a cabinet just inside the kitchen. If things went south, he wanted to be prepared. He hadn't asked anyone to give up what weapons they carried but Lori, Helena, and Jacob had done so before dinner on their own. For the time being, Thomas had tossed them all onto his bed upstairs and they were well out of reach in a crisis. It was a stupid thing to do in hindsight. The only other weapons remotely close by were the rifle and shotgun he kept near the front and back doors.

Lori bent over Elijah as Jacob directed her to the skin of the man's cheek just below the freaky goggles he wore. She jumped at what she saw there, bumping into the coffee table, as she retreated. "Jacob's right. I can't believe it but he's telling the truth." Lori's voice was thick with fear.

Thomas thought she might even have turned a

touch pale. "So what does it mean?"

"Don't ask me, mate!" Jacob whirled on him.

"He told me he was on a military base when the rotter plague started. I assumed he was, like you know, a colonel or something. What if he was an experiment? Maybe even patient zero for the virus and it got loose when he did?" Lori trembled as she went on. "Or maybe he's some kind of super soldier they were developing. You've seen him fight."

"You watched too much TV, didn't you?" Thomas shook his head. "There's got to be a more rational explanation.

"Maybe he really is just sick," Helena offered.

"And maybe I am bloody Superman!" Jacob spat at her.

Thomas wanted to move between the two of them. To be honest, he wanted to punch the jerk writer into next week but he stayed where he was, close to the pistol. "Settle down, boy. This is my house and I can toss you out of it as easy as I let you in. I hope you understand that."

Lori must have regained her nerve because she leaned over Elijah and gently removed his goggles. Underneath, his face was as normal looking as anybody else's.

"He always wore these things. Why? Have any of you ever seen his eyes?" she asked.

Neither Jacob nor Helena answered her.

"Maybe he was hiding them."

"They seem pretty normal to me," Jacob scoffed.

"They're not open, you idiot!" Lori yelled at him.

Thomas felt feel the tension in the room like a tangible force

"Open them," he ordered her. "If you think it's such a big deal, do it and find out?"

Thomas got the pistol out of the drawer, shoving it into the back of his pants, under his shirt, and moved to watch over Lori's shoulder as she reached with her fingertips and parted the lids over Elijah's left eye.

Beneath it was a pool of black. There was no iris or pupil, not even any white on the edges, only darkness that moved and swirled about like the waters of an ocean stirred by the wind.

Lori cried out as Elijah's hand shot up, his fingers closing around her wrist. Thomas met Elijah's gaze as those midnight orbs looked up at him. His insides went cold, his heart skipping a beat.

"Why?" Elijah asked. "Why did you do this?"

"What are you?" Thomas asked.

Next to him, Helena squealed.

"We're sorry, Elijah. We were worried about you. We owe you so much," she wailed.

Elijah released Lori, sitting up on the couch. "You want to know what I am, Thomas?"

Thomas took a step away from as Elijah spoke.

"Do you really want to know?" Elijah pressed him.

Thomas changed his question. "Are you the reason the rotters exist?"

"No," Elijah answered. "I am no more responsible for the rotters than you are. In fact, I am trying to escape them. That's why I came here. Did your father ever tell you about the night the lights fell from the sky?"

Thomas shook his head.

"Your grandfather was a good man, Thomas. He died well on his feet and fighting. I'm sorry it had to be that way but I had to hide you see? Your government knew I was here and they were coming for me."

Thomas was totally confused and still not sure he was buying the crap Elijah was pouring out onto him. They made some pretty fancy contact lenses and Elijah was moving with the jerking tics of a crazy person as he explained himself.

"You're saying you knew my grandfather, that you killed him? Did I hear that part right?"

"None of that matters, Thomas. It's all so long ago. I was forced to leave something on your farm, though, and I am afraid I'll be needing it back now."

"Take it and go," Thomas told him. "I don't want there to be any more trouble than there has to be."

"He can't just go, can you, Elijah?" Lori said.

It was Elijah's turn to shake his head. "I am sorry but she's right. If by some slim chance you survive, your race survives, I can't leave the knowledge of my existence as a known fact."

"So you mean no witnesses?" Jacob asked, already appearing to know the answer.

Elijah's hand moved so fast it became a blur before Thomas's eyes. A throwing knife flashed as it flew through the air to bury itself in the flesh of Jacob's throat. Jacob made horrible, sickening, gurgling noises as blood bubbled up and out of his open mouth. He was still trying to pull the knife from his throat as he died and sank to the floor with a dull thud.

"Yes, that about sums it up," Elijah said as Thomas made his move. The farmer brought the pistol around, putting three rounds into Elijah's chest. Elijah was flung into the couch behind him from their impact as yellow blood splashed over the front of his trench coat from the wounds.

"You killed him!" Lori shouted.

"He killed Jacob!" Helena screamed. She fell to her knees beside Jacob's corpse, cradling his head in her lap. Bright red blood was still bubbling out of the hole in his neck. It ran over the tanned skin of her thighs and stained the long T-shirt she wore.

"I sure hope so," Thomas yelled at Lori. Some sort of smoke grenade popped as it rolled onto the floor from Elijah's hand. The fog-like cloud it produced burnt Thomas's eyes. He fired off two more shots at where he thought Elijah had to be. Lori and Helena were screaming bloody murder.

"Get to the kitchen!" he shouted at them, even though he couldn't see them. He hoped visibility would be clearer in the other room. He heard them banging and bumping around as they tried to make their way there. He whammed his wounded leg on the coffee table as he spun to make a run for it himself and went sprawling onto the floor, his eyes tearing up even more from the pain. Thomas didn't attempt to get up. Instead, pulling himself along with his hands, he crawled out of the smoke onto the house's front porch. Gulping in the fresh air, he used the porch's railing to haul himself to his feet, favoring his wounded leg as he stood.

Duke and Hunter met him as he limped down the porch's steps into the yard. "Go get him, boys!" he ordered them. They charged into the house through the open front door, barking and snarling as they went. Thomas hoped the dogs would buy them some time. His plan was to head around the house to the backdoor and join Helena and Lori in the kitchen. He prayed that they had made it. Elijah wasn't human, that much was clear. Still, three point blank rounds to the chest surely would slow him down some. As good a warrior as Elijah appeared to be, what if the man had been holding back so that no one would suspect what he really was? That thought really terrified Thomas.

He heard one of the dogs cry out with a high pitched whine. It cut deep to his soul. Those dogs were his best friends, but they were also trained guard dogs and they would put up a fight as was their duty. Then there was no sound but his own ragged breathing as he rounded the corner of the house, nearly colliding with Helena and Lori. They were as startled as he was.

"Oh, Thomas!" Helena flung herself into his

arms. He saw Lori had the shotgun he kept by the kitchen door in her hands.

"What the Hell are we going to do?" Lori asked.

"I don't know," Thomas shrugged, "but you can bet Elijah's going to be coming after us."

"L-O-R-I! T-H-O-M-A-S!" they heard Elijah calling to them, "Where are you? Don't you want to play?"

"That guy is one sick—" Thomas started.

Lori stuck up a hand, telling him to shut up.

"I'm not going into the woods," Helena whispered into Thomas's ear as he held her to him.

The second floor window above them exploded outward as Elijah came leaping through it. Glass rained over them. Thomas raised an arm to block it and keep it from hitting Helena.

Elijah landed like a cat, a few feet from where they stood. Lori slung her shotgun around, squeezing the trigger. Elijah sidestepped its blast, closing in on them. Thomas shoved Helena away from him. "Run!" he ordered her as Elijah drew his swords. Lori's shotgun jammed. She was still struggling to chamber another round as Thomas opened fire. His Glock spat four shots at Elijah in rapid succession. Elijah swatted the bullets from the air like they were moving in slow motion. A shower of sparks dancing on the blades of his swords. Elijah grinned as Thomas stared at him in awe. Elijah sprang forward. One of his blades sent the Glock flying from Thomas' hand. His other sword was streaking towards Thomas' neck as Lori's shotgun thundered again. It blew a gaping hole in Elijah's side and sent him rolling into the dirt. Thomas stood watching him writhe in pain as Elijah tried to reach one of his throwing knives. Lori's hand clamped on Thomas's wrist, pulling him out of his shock, as she tugged on him, trying to drag him into action.

"We have to move!" she shouted in his face. Thomas took off after her as she sprinted for the house's backdoor. She led him inside and up the stairs to his bedroom. Slamming its door and locking it, Lori rushed to glance out the window at the yard below. "I don't see him. He's gone," she said, but Thomas was only half listening. He ripped the closet door open.

"I never thought I would have to use this," he told her as he produced a well kept AK-47 from its depths and checked the rifle's magazine.

"Thank God for rednecks and their toys," Lori said.

"Wait," Thomas said, "Where is Helena?"

Helena ran down the driveway towards the gate heading into the road. The gravel poked at and scraped the bare soles of her feet making her wince with each step. The truck wasn't too far away. She remembered that Thomas had left a rifle in it. If she could just reach it and get the gun, maybe she could work up the courage to go back to the house and see if Thomas and Lori were okay.

The gate, unlike the rest of the fence, wasn't electrified. She thanked God for that fact as she tripped and stumbled into it. Cold fingers reached through it to stroke the skin of her cheek. Helena screamed, flinging herself backwards onto the ground. She had been so focused on running away from Elijah, she hadn't realized what she was running towards. Dozens upon dozens of rotters were pressed against the outside of the gate and along the length of the fence, trying to force their way through it. Dozens more fried, crispy corpses lay at their feet. The first wave of rotters had shorted out the fence and soon these new ones would tear their way inside using the strength of their sheer numbers. There were so many of the things, and even more coming, staggering along the road to join the throngs at the fence. The rotters had followed them home. Their moans were hungry, desperate, and loud.

"Hello, Helena," Elijah said from somewhere behind her.

She pushed herself to her feet, turning around to face him. Elijah looked to be hurting. One of his hands was held tight against a wound on his side that oozed yellow blood, dripping onto the rocks of the driveway.

"Elijah, please . . ." she begged him. "I don't care what you are. You saved me."

"We seem to be drawing quite a large amount of unwanted attention," he commented, glancing at the rotters.

"Please," she whispered again.

"I can't have them getting in yet," he said, "and there's too many to simply kill alone."

He stepped to her. "Looks like I need a, what do you call it, a distraction, eh?"

"What?" Helena asked, not knowing what he meant. Elijah grabbed her, lifting her from the ground. Helena screamed as Elijah tossed her through the air over the fence into the waiting mass of dead men and women. Fingernails tore at her flesh and teeth ripped chunks of meat from her body. She felt waves of teeth sink into her muscles. She kept right on screaming until a gaunt, teenage rotter leaned over her, as if to kiss her mouth, and bit out her tongue.

"**I** don't know where Helena is," Lori answered Thomas. "You told her to run."

"We've got to go find her," Thomas said, starting for the bedroom door.

"You do that and we're all dead. Think about it, Thomas. As fast as Elijah is, out there we're sitting ducks."

"And we're not in here?" he countered.

"In here, there's only two ways he can come at us, the window and the door. At least we know where to watch for him. Out there, he could take us both with a little luck before we even knew what was happening."

Thomas took a seat on the edge of the bed, defeated. Lori's logic was too sound to argue with. "What is he?"

"Weren't you listening?" Lori snapped at him. "He's a freaking alien like from the X-files or some crap."

"What's the X-files?"

"Forget it." Lori reloaded her shotgun from a box of shells that was sitting on the night table beside the bed. "He's an alien, an E.T., whatever you want to call it and he's trying to go home."

"How?" Thomas asked.

"Based on what he said, he left something here years ago that he needs to get home. That's why he brought us all here. Maybe some kind of emergency beacon to call for help. Heck, for all I know his ship could be buried under this farm."

"If that's the case, then aren't we already screwed? It'd tear through this house like rocks through paper as it took off. Wouldn't it?"

"I'm just guessing, Thomas. I'm just as lost as you are."

"I don't think he has a ship," Thomas said after a couple of seconds. "He said something about bright lights falling from the sky. I bet he crashed his ship when he got here. Besides, if he had a ship, wouldn't he be gone already? I know I would."

"You mean aside from the fact that he wants us dead?" Lori pointed out.

"Yeah," Thomas managed a weak grin, "Aside from that, you figure he would be gone."

They stared at each other in silence again.

"I hope Helena's okay," Thomas said.

"Me too," Lori agreed as the screaming started outside.

Elijah stood watching the rotters feasting on Helena. Two of the things were fighting over a strand of her intestines. He felt a pang of guilt at killing the girl but he reminded himself that the humans were expendable and now that they knew what he was, they needed to die. He had only gathered them and brought them along to be used as cannon fodder against the dead anyway. A moving shield whose purpose was to help him get this far unharmed. In this respect, Helena was serving her purpose very well. He spun and ran with the speed of a cheetah towards the house. The transmitter had to be in its cellar somewhere. He had to find it and send a call for extraction. Elijah refused to die on this primitive and worthless world. Humans were a vile, selfish, confused, and violent race that deserved to be extinct. The rotters would surely see to it that they would be too. He'd seen viruses like this one in his travels before. It was a rare and miraculous thing for any species to survive this type of plague. Far more advanced races had already fallen to things like this virus. Humanity was no match for it.

Elijah stumbled as he reached the porch. The

woman had hurt him more than he had thought. The tissues of his body were weaving together and closing the wound quickly, like they had the ones to his chest, but not fast enough for his liking. He could smell the remaining two humans above him, upstairs, but there would be time for them later. The sooner he found the transmitter and sent out the call for help, the better. It might take some time for a ship to arrive and time was something he was running out of. It wouldn't be long until the fence gave way to the rotters' sheer numbers and he didn't relish the thought of making a last stand in this house. If it came to that however, he would seal himself in the cellar and hope its thick wooden doors would hold the creatures at bay long enough for his trip home to arrive.

He pushed through the house, stepped over the two lifeless dogs, leaving drops of yellow blood in his wake. The cellar was damp and musty. There was no source of light, only total darkness, but he didn't need one. The blackness was as bright as the mid-day sun to his eyes. He sniffed the air, searching for the transmitter's bitter, metallic scent. At last, he found it. His fist punched through the cement blocks of the cellar's wall and he removed it from the dirt behind the wall. A smile parted his lips as he flipped it on, heard its familiar hum, sending a desperate cry for help into the stars. He carefully placed it in the center of the cellar's floor to keep broadcasting its signal, then headed upstairs to finish things with the humans while he waited.

◉◉◉

"**We** can't keep just waiting here," Thomas complained.

"You got a better plan?" Lori asked.

"That was Helena screaming a few minutes ago or don't you care?"

"I didn't exactly see you running to help her."

"You told me to stay here!" Thomas leapt up from the bed. Lori looked like she expected him to hit her. Thomas reigned in his anger and tried to calm himself. "If she's dead, Lori. . ."

"I am sorry, Thomas, but you know she is. She didn't stand a chance out there alone and we wouldn't either."

A chorus of moans arose from the yard below them. Together they rushed to the window.

"Oh, my holy. . ." Thomas muttered as they stared at an army of rotting bodies shambling up the driveway towards the house. There was a hundred or more of the things and there was no doubt as to why they were coming.

"They must have broken through the fence," Lori said.

"Really?" Thomas snapped, fully losing what control he had left. "You think? I figured Elijah must have just let them in." He said cruelly, knowing Elijah was threatened as much by the monsters as they were.

"Well, this certainly changes things." Lori started grabbing handfuls of shells for her shotgun and ramming them into the pockets of her jeans. Thomas loaded up on ammo and other weapons too, tucking a pistol under his belt and slinging a high powered hunting rifle onto his shoulder by its strap. He kept the AK-47 as his primary weapon. There wasn't a lot of ammo for it. He only had the clip in the gun and three other mags for it but if Elijah came calling, they would need its firepower.

Lori eased open the bedroom door. The hallway was clear. The smell of bacon still lingered in the air. "Do we make for the woods or the truck?"

"The woods," Thomas said firmly. "If we make it, we can always wait for the rotters to settle down and wander off. The truck will still be there when they do."

"Crap," Lori said. Thomas followed her gaze, seeing that the front door leading into the living room was open. A fat, dead man came lumbering inside through it. He was shirtless and rolls of gray flesh jiggled with each step he took, shaking loose scores of the maggots crawling over him onto the floor. Thomas could see more rotters approaching in the yard. He resisted the urge to make some kind of snide remark like *they're here*.

"Backdoor," Lori said, apparently already far ahead of him. They raced down the stairs. The fat man caught sight of them and snarled, showing tobacco- and blood-stained teeth. Thomas dropped him with a burst to his head before he got close enough to be a threat. The noise of the shots drove the rotters outside into a frenzy. Thomas cursed himself for being too jumpy as a stream of the creatures poured through the open front door. Both Thomas and Lori were taken off guard as Elijah fell from where he'd been waiting for them on the ceiling into the rotters. His swords twirling, he sent the three rotters who had already made their way inside to Hell and kicked the front door shut with one of his heavy boots.

"I believe we have some business to conclude," he grinned at them.

Thomas clicked the AK-47 into full auto. Elijah was already moving as he squeezed the gun's trigger. It chattered, spitting spent casing to clatter and roll across the floor.

Elijah jumped upwards, reattaching himself to the ceiling like some kind of bug. He skittered across it towards them with a speed too fast for Thomas to match. Lori was ready though. The blast from her shotgun tore away Elijah's right arm at the elbow, causing him to lose his grip. His body thudded against the hard wood of the floor a few feet from where they stood.

"Yeah!" Thomas howled. "Take that, you freak!"

Elijah's left hand threw a knife before either of them saw it coming. The blade slashed Lori's left arm deeply as it passed her. She screamed from the pain as the shotgun went flying from her hands. Thomas swung his AK-47, trying to get another shot at Elijah, but the freak was already gone. A trail of yellow blood led to the cellar door. Thomas heard it slam shut.

"He's locked himself in!" Thomas shouted.

"Who cares?" Lori yelled. "Let's get the heck of out of here!"

Again, he had faced the humans and again somehow they had beaten him at his own game. The woman's shot was blind luck. It could have been nothing else. Elijah gripped the railing of the stairs as he half stumbled down them into the cellar. His yellow blood glowed in the shadows of the room. This time there was light but he paid no attention to that fact. His wound was too severe to fully heal. Not even his body could regrow an entire new hand. Elijah decided to cut his losses. No matter where on this filthy planet the humans fled, the rotters would be there, waiting. In the end, they would die. As he slumped against the cellar wall, he noticed the light and realized something was very, very wrong. The huge double doors of the cellar's bulkhead, leading out to the house's backyard, lay in pieces on the dirt floor. There was a deep, rumbling chuff nearby. It rode on a thick scent of musk that burned his nostrils.

The sasquatch.

He knew it was here, in the cellar with him. He craned his neck to glance at the rows of shelves near the rear of the cellar. The beast squatted there as motionless as a statue, its breathing steady and controlled. Like him, the beast appeared to be bloodied and exhausted. Trying to escape the rotters, it must have come here seeking shelter.

Elijah and the beast stared at each other, eyes of blackness meeting orbs of burning yellow. He slowly eased one of the pistols under his trench coat from its holster. *So close to going home,* he thought. He wrapped a finger around the trigger, trying to move quickly but quietly.

Then the beast roared, crawling on its hands and knees towards him because the cellar's ceiling was too low for it to stand. Elijah's first shot turned its right eye into pulp, leaving an empty socket and spouting blood in its place. He never had time to fire a second. A massive, hair-covered hand crushed his skull against the cement blocks of the wall behind him. The last thing Elijah heard was the sound of his own bones breaking and blood rushing outward to fill his ears.

Lori beat him into the kitchen but Thomas caught up to her as she skidded to a halt at the backdoor. Thomas saw the crumpled and twisted bodies of over twenty rotters strewn across the backyard. They had deep gouges in their faces. "The beast," he panted, trying to catch his breath. His leg was killing him. He didn't dare look at it. He knew what he would see. Thomas could feel fresh blood trickling along the length of his leg and the pool of warm liquid sloshing around in his boot. All the movement and the fighting had not only re-opened the long gash running from the top of his boot to his knee but it felt like it had made it worse. He saw concern in Lori's eyes as she looked at him. "If it's out there, we're dead. We can't fight the rotters and it too," he told her.

"We're dead already, Thomas."

Thomas shook his head. "There's always hope as long as we're still breathing."

"You ready?" she asked.

"No." Thomas straightened himself up, standing as tall as he could on his wounded leg. "I'm not running anymore."

"We don't have time for this," Lori pleaded.

"I mean it," Thomas said, "This is my home. If I'm going to die, I'll die here like my dad did."

He could tell Lori didn't know what to say.

"Guess this is where we part ways then," he said for her.

"Guess so," she said sadly. "Keep fighting, Thomas. Life is too precious just to give up on," With that, she was gone through the backdoor. He didn't bother to watch her running across the yard. Thomas loaded a fresh mag into his rifle. His plan was to make it upstairs to his bedroom again. There, he'd make his last stand. Either he would kill all the rotters in and around the house or he would run out of ammo and the things would finally get the meal they were after. What happened to him now was in God's hand and he made his peace with that.

Lori sprinted for the trees. A handful of rotters emerged from them, racing to meet her. The less noise she made, the better so she took a page from Elijah's book of tricks. A dead woman with a belly swollen and distended, either from gas or her last meal, came barreling at her. Lori swung her shotgun like a club. Its butt slammed into the side of the woman's head with the cracking sound of fracturing bone. The woman rolled into the grass and lay there twitching as Lori ran past her. A snarling guy, dressed in National Guard combat fatigues, came at her from her side. She thrust the shotgun's butt forward to meet his chin, shattering his jaw and sending him staggering backwards from the impact of the blow. Lori was only a few yards from the treeline when the beast came tearing out of the cellar beneath Thomas' house with an earthshaking roar.

"Frag me," she muttered, pouring on all the extra speed her exhausted body could muster. It came bounding after her, crushing skulls and sweeping the remaining rotters from its path like they were nothing more than children's toys. Lori ducked a low tree limb as she burst into the woods. She wasn't so stupid as to think she could lose the beast in the trees like she had planned to do with the rotters. These woods were its home and it was a heck of a lot smarter and more cunning than those sacks of decaying meat on two legs. It was faster too. As she reached the fence that surrounded the farm, she knew she was going to have to stand and fight. She could hear the beast knocking over trees as it rushed through the woods after her. Pumping a fresh round into the shotgun's chamber, she turned to face it. One of its huge hands was reaching for her. She noticed one of its eyes was gone, replaced by an empty socket. Blood still flowed from the wound, matting the beast's hair to its cheek in a sticky mess of congealing red.

Lori sidestepped its extended hand, moving closer to the monster. The barrel of her shotgun made contact with the flesh of its throat as she pulled the trigger. The shotgun bucked in her hands as the point blank blast blew a gaping hole between the beast's chin and its chest. The beast stopped, its breath wheezing through what remained of the windpipe dangling from the mangled mess of its throat. It raised one hand to cover the lethal wound, trying to stop the spray of blood that rained down over her where she stood under it. Its other hand caught her with a backhanded slap as she turned to run. She felt pain and something snap inside of her as the blow lifted her from her feet, sending her twisting through the air to land in the grass several feet away.

Lori lay on the ground, her top half facing one direction, her bottom half another, as she watched the beast collapse. A pool of blood forming around the beast's unmoving head. Lori couldn't feel her legs but the pain in her spine was so intense it was like hellfire melting away her flesh. She tried to right herself and roll fully over onto her back but the pain made it impossible. As the world began to spin around her and her vision blurred there was movement in the trees. A trio of rotters, either drawn to her by the noise of the shotgun's blast or the smell of all the blood, closed in on her. She tried to scream as one grabbed her by her long hair, yanking her head to the side, but all that came out was a pathetic whimpering sound. She felt another of the creatures sink its teeth into her side, digging into the meat of her stomach as the first one tore a chunk of her shoulder away. The last thing Lori saw was the third rotter wandering away, carrying the gnawed-off lower part of one of her legs.

Thomas hosed the rotters in the living room on full auto, emptying his entire clip in a single stream of continuous fire. An elderly man missing most of his face took numerous rounds to his shoulders and chest, flopping over the couch. Thomas' bullets splattered brain matter onto the wall from a topless, teenage blonde in a cheerleader's skirt onto the room's wall. A solider with his insides spilling from a hole in his gut spun to crash on top of the coffee table, taking more rounds than Thomas could even guess at. All around the room the dead fell. Only a few were put down permanently but all that mattered to Thomas was buying time. He popped out the empty clip, shoving in a new one as he limped for the stairs, leaving a trail of warm red from his wounded leg in his wake. As he reached the bottom of the stairs, he hosed the entire area of the living room again until his rifle clicked empty once more. Thomas hauled his exhausted and hurting body up the steps as he loaded his last mag. More rotters were pouring through the open front door of the house. Thomas ignored them until he hit the top of the stairs. Only then did he turn to fire on them as they bounded up the steps after him. He spent over half his last clip buying some breathing room, sending the faster of the creatures tumbling down the steps to trip up and block the next wave behind them.

Thomas hobbled into his bedroom, slamming its door closed. He tossed his Ak-47 aside, snatching up a .38 revolver and a Glock from the pile of weapons on the bed. Shoving the remaining weapons out of his way, he plopped onto the edge of the bed. He paid no attention to the sound of dead fists pounding on the door as it shook in its frame. His leg was throbbing. Thomas shut his eyes and tried to push the pain from his mind. The plan was a simple one. He had plenty of weapons and ammo and the dead could only enter the bedroom one or two at a time. If he kept his cool and the blood loss from his leg didn't get him, he should be able to kill the entire pack of the things that had followed them home. He guessed there were less than a hundred of the rotters and not all of them were inside the house yet. Steady, he told himself, you can do this, as the door rattled from the rotters' continued attack on it.

Cracks formed and grew in the wood of the door. Finally, with a loud crash, it splintered and broke open. Thomas aimed his shots carefully. His first shot sent a punk kid in a Snoop Dog T-shirt back to Hell. His second sprayed brain matter and pus-like blood from the skull of a once hot redhead in a mini-skirt into the air. One after another, the rotters fell, creating a barricade of corpses that helped him by slowing down the ones trying to shove their way into the room over them. As soon as one gun clicked empty, Thomas discarded it, replacing it with another from the pile beside him on the bed. Soon the room was filled with gun smoke and the stench of blood and rotting entrails. The number of rotters at the door dwindled to where he could see past them into the hall.

Then, a high pitched screeching filled the room, coming from somewhere outside, above the roof of the house. It was so intense, Thomas had no choice but to drop his weapons and clasp his hands over his ears. Whatever it was, the noise was affecting the rotters as well. Thomas watched a woman missing her nose stop in the doorway of the bedroom, swaying back and forth, as black pus oozed from eyes and ears, as if the noise was crushing her brain inside her skull. The ceiling above him burst into flames, the heat so intense the wood disintegrated into tiny flecks of ash that drifted in the air, swirling about like black snow. Thomas looked through the hole in the ceiling, up into the sky. A gleaming, silver cylinder the size of a small plane hovered over the house. As he stared at it in horror, a wide beam of bright blue energy erupted from its center and speared down to encase him. Thomas screamed, trying to reach for another gun, then he was simply gone.

The cylinder hovered above the house for a few more seconds before it shot diagonally upwards through the sky, leaving the rotters, the house, the dying beast in the woods, and the Earth behind.

EPILOGUE

Thomas awoke with a start. His instincts told him he was drowning. He was inside some sort of transparent tube filled with a clear liquid too greasy to be water. He tried to hold his breath, thrashing and smacking his hands against the transparent glass of the tube. Thomas could feel the liquid coating his eyes. It seeped into his mouth and nose as he finally had no choice but to try to breathe. As the liquid reached his lungs, it somehow provided oxygen to his cells. The process was horrifying but he wasn't drowning. His rational brain waged a war with the more primitive part of his mind to convince his body that it was okay and there was no danger. He stopped struggling and floated in the liquid.

The room around the tube that held him was like the interior of a cave, only the walls weren't made of rock. They had a shimmering, organic appearance, as if he were Jonah and this place was the belly of the whale that had swallowed him. Everything was illuminated by an eerie green light that seemed to come from everywhere at once. Thomas remembered the strange blue beam shining onto him and the tingling sensation that had swept over his entire body. He lost control of his bladder, urinating into the liquid of the tube that held him. Streams of yellow bubbled by his eyes.

He was on a spaceship, the cylinder-like craft he had seen above his house.

A section of the wall separated like two cells dividing under a microscope and something entered the room. The wall merged together again behind it, a mass of knitting tissues. The thing had three legs, spider-like in appearance. Above them was a malformed—by human standards anyway—twisted torso that resembled a human turned sideways with arms protruding from what would have been the human's front and back. Each of the arms ended in a nine fingered hand. The fingers were elongated. He counted four joints on each of them. The thing's head, however, was remarkably like a human's, the only differences being the lack of hair and the twin orbs of flowing darkness where its eyes should be. It screeched at him.

When his only response was a stunned look of terror, it stuck out its tongue, which split into three tentacles before withdrawing into its mouth once more. This time when it spoke, it did so in perfect English. "Your designation is Thomas Hyatt, is it not?"

Thomas nodded.

"I would ask you where the man you knew as Elijah was but I don't suppose it matters. The XZH virus is loose on your world so it is of no further use to us. Any information he managed to gain about your race is now useless as it will be extinct in a matter of days if it isn't already."

The alien's side slid open. One of its hands reached into the new pocket and produced something that looked very much like a scalpel. "Still, I suppose for protocol's sake we should at least take a look inside you and see what makes you tick."

Thomas tried to scream but the viscous liquid choked his vocal chords silent.

Author Bio

Eric S. Brown is the author of numerous books including the *Bigfoot War* series, *War of the Worlds Plus Blood Guts and Zombies, How the West Went to Hell, Season of Rot,* and *World War of the Dead* to name only a few. His short fiction has been published hundreds of times in the small press and beyond. He lives in North Carolina with his family where he continues to writes tales of blazing guns, hungry corpses, and the things that lurk in the woods.

www.ingramcontent.com/pod-product-compliance
Lightning Source LLC
Chambersburg PA
CBHW022029170626
46808CB00003B/1109